For Sonia —

with all

best wishes,

*The
River
of Lost
Voices*

The

Iowa

Short

Fiction

Award

University of

Iowa Press

Iowa City

Mark Brazaitis

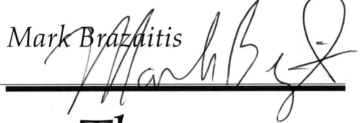

The
River
of Lost
Voices

Stories from Guatemala

University of Iowa Press, Iowa City 52242

Copyright © 1998 by Mark Brazaitis

Printed in the United States of America

http://www.uiowa.edu/~uipress

Printed on acid-free paper

Library of Congress Cataloging-in-Publication Data

Brazaitis, Mark

The river of lost voices: stories from Guatemala /

Mark Brazaitis.

p.   cm.—(Iowa short fiction award)

ISBN 0-87745-642-9 (pbk.)

1. Guatemala—Social life and customs—Fiction.

2. Indians of Central America—Guatemala—Fiction.

3. Mountain life—Guatemala—Fiction.   I. Title.

II. Series.

PS3552.R3566R58   1998

813'.54—dc21   98-24437

98 99 00 01 02 P 5 4 3 2 1

to the people of Santa Cruz Verapaz,

Guatemala, especially María Argelia Caál

Caál, Alida Beatriz Catalán Güe, Ingrid

Dricela Rax Rodríguez, and Pablo César

Rax Rodríguez

and to my mother, father, and sister

Contents

ACKNOWLEDGMENTS

No work is entirely an author's own. I am indebted to the following people who have supported my writing over the years: my grandparents, Martin and Lella Loftus and Regina Brazaitis; my parents, Sheila Loftus and Tom Brazaitis; my stepfather, Jim Eddinger; my sister, Sarah Jean Brazaitis; my stepbrother Eddie Clift; my teachers Lewis Hyde, Richard Messer, Robert Early, Philip O'Connor, and Howard McCord; my friends Elsa Arnett, Jessica Dorman, and Howard and Karen Owen; my adviser and advocate, John Coyne; my colleague and racquetball partner, David Hassler; and my wife, Julie Penn, whose enthusiasm, understanding, and love have been this writer's blessing.

I also would like to thank the editors of the journals in which some of the stories in this collection first appeared: "Snow" and "How They Healed," *Beloit Fiction Journal*; "A Detective's Story," *Chattahoochee Review*; "The Liar," *Western Humanities Review*; "The Whale," *Pennsylvania Review*; "The Corner Kick," *Greensboro Review*; "Bathwater," *Alaska Quarterly Review*; and "Gemelas," *Hawai'i Review*.

José del Río

I was born dead and I've never been allowed to forget it. Nor would I want to. Because I was not supposed to live, my life has been a freak occasion, free of obligation. I am a ghost and I enjoy a ghost's freedom.

I was not supposed to live. God left me in the dark room with my mother, wet and lifeless in her arms. The women who had come to help with my birth cried, and my father turned away and walked to the cantina. My mother said a hundred prayers, then fell silent, with no more prayers to say. The women went away, and my mother slept with me in her lap. I woke her with my first breath.

The women came back the next morning to celebrate a miracle, and my father, still drunk, lifted me and kissed me with cantina kisses. But that night my mother held me in her arms and whispered her amazement and fear: "I dreamed of a river and a serpent and I heard you breathe."

My father wanted to name me Lazarus and the women all suggested variations of "del Milagro," but my mother named me José del Río after her brother, who at age thirty-two drowned while swimming in the shallow river on the far side of town.

I owed nothing to God. Mine was a free life, a freak life. I was supposed to be dead.

Everyone thought I was retarded because I didn't say a word until I was fifteen years old. Concerned about the forbidding influence I might have on my three sisters, my father consigned me to a room in the front of our house. My sisters, all older than I, slept in a back room across the courtyard. They acknowledged me only when they brought new friends home and pointed me out as a zookeeper would an exotic animal: "He was born dead."

Around town, however, I was celebrated as a mentally deficient angel, one to whom everyone turned as living proof of God's existence. "Here he is, the boy who was born dead, the one our Savior rescued." Because of my sacred status, my father liked to keep me beside him whenever we had visitors.

My father was an assistant to the mayor in those days, and our house was used as a meeting place by local government and military officials. In addition to their official positions, many of these men were owners of plantations. Their coffee plants lined the mountains around town like fat, green-uniformed soldiers. My father, though, was not wealthy enough to own a plantation; instead, he planted corn on land he rented in a nearby village. But my father's voice—more radiant and powerful than a priest's—helped him overcome his low status. Because of his voice, he was, at these gatherings, a kind of master of ceremonies.

On meeting nights, my mother and sisters were sent to church or to my aunt's house. I was permitted to stay, my father always informing everyone, unnecessarily, that they needn't fear my presence because "a wall couldn't keep a secret better." My father would inaugurate each meeting by asking the men to place their guns on the table. Everyone would be silent a moment, staring at the sparkling collection of black and silver. "Well," my father would say. "Here, *caballeros*, is power." My father would lift his arms, the men would reclaim their guns, and the meeting would begin.

Between discussions of life and death, the men swigged beer and traded uncouth comments about local women. One night, a little drunk, as usual, my father described his seduction of Doña Blanca; because of his intoxication and her girth, he said, he'd needed her help in "finding the entrance." Lieutenant Rubio told of a similar experience with the same woman and declared, "I wasn't even drunk."

During one of these meetings, Mayor Gualim spoke bitterly about Miguel Cal, the owner of a sawmill. Don Miguel gave scraps of wood to plantation workers for their fires and explained to them, leaning out the window above the mountain of sawdust where they all gathered, that a plantation owner was legally obliged to pay the minimum wage of five quetzales a day, not half that, as was custom in our town. "He's a guerrilla," Mayor Gualim said. Grinning, Lieutenant Rubio asked the mayor if Don Miguel's political ambitions—he was known to be considering a race for mayor in the next election—also concerned him. Mayor Gualim said, "What concerns me is the purity of our town." He winked, and Lieutenant Rubio laughed. Then the room fell silent and the two men stared at each other, their grins gone.

"When?" Mayor Gualim asked.

On the night Don Miguel was supposed to die, I waited in his yard. Don Miguel's house had a big front window that looked in on his television, and people from town would often gather outside to watch without sound whatever Don Miguel was watching. Don Miguel's wife was dead and his two sons were grown and living in the capital, but he had recently bought a swing set and slide, which children in town had christened already with muddy feet.

I was sitting on a swing, about twenty meters from the front of the house, when Lieutenant Rubio and two soldiers pulled up in a van and knocked on the door. When Don Miguel answered, asking in an anxious voice what the men wanted, one soldier jabbed his rifle into Don Miguel's stomach. Don Miguel bent over, clutching himself, then fell on his knees. No one moved for a long time. Finally, Don Miguel looked up. The second soldier placed the end of his rifle between Don Miguel's eyes and pulled the trigger. The sound was softer than a dog's bark. The two soldiers dragged Don Miguel's body to the van as Lieutenant Rubio entered the house. In a few minutes, he returned outside and stepped into the van.

When I could no longer see the van or hear its motor, I walked into the house. In the living room, the cushions of the couch had been removed and thrown aside, and a glass cabinet next to the television had been cleared of its objects. Ceramic figures and soccer trophies lay broken on the floor. Down a hallway, in Don Miguel's bedroom, the mattress had been removed from the frame and the drawers of his dresser pulled open. A single black sock hung like a burned tongue from the top drawer.

In the last room at the end of the hall, a *bodega* full of old machetes, hoes, and scraps of wood, I smelled wax. There was no light switch, but the moonlight from the small break between the block walls and tin roof provided enough light to see. I moved past the tools and wood to the back of the room, where I saw a small desk in the corner. There was a candle on the desk; touching it, I felt the still soft wax.

Below the candle was a sheet of paper with neat numbers filling a hand-drawn column on the right edge. Don Miguel obviously had been counting his money, but the interruption had forced him to conceal it. He had not, however, done a thorough job. The end of a new bill stuck out of the bottom drawer. Opening the drawer, I reached in and pulled out a fistful of tens. Deeper in the drawer were stacks of twenties and fifties, each held together by thick rubber bands.

I was not permitted to eat with my father, mother, and sisters, so I ate on my bed, where my mother would join me after serving everyone. My mother was a tall, thin woman who wore only black or dark blue *corte*, although my father was *ladino* and wore blue jeans and cowboy hats.

My mother always smelled like wood smoke from her cooking fire. Even her breath smelled and felt like smoke, fragrant and warm. Sitting next to me, my mother would wrap her hands in her *corte* and talk to me as if I could understand. She spoke to me in Spanish, in order, she said, to prepare me to survive in the modern world, although when she got tired, she would drop, dreamlike, into Pokomchí. I loved the way the words clicked in her throat.

Often she would ask me questions. "What do you think of the new outhouse your father built?" She would wait for a response, smiling patiently. "He's good with his hands," she would continue. "His father was a carpenter, you know. Do you think his father would approve of what he does?"

Sometimes late at night, my mother would leave her bedroom and walk across the courtyard to visit me. Often it would be raining, and even minutes after she had sat next to me on my bed, water would trickle from her hair. She told me the stories her mother had told her, the fables of our town. She always apologized before beginning a story, explaining that her mother knew the story better. Her mother, she said, told these stories over and over and hardly altered a word from one telling to the next, her fidelity like a priest's to the Bible. My mother told the stories softly, with a whistle in her voice like a wind tickling tree branches. I liked best the story about the two priests and the serpent, and my mother must have known because she told this story more often than the others.

"A long time ago," my mother would begin, "not long after the Spanish came to our town and built the church, there were two priests who hoarded the church's money, gold and silver coins stacked as high as their eyes, in a room at the back of the church. At the end of every night, even on nights they gave mass, the priests would retreat to their room at the back of the church to count the money. One would count silver, the other gold. Then they would trade jobs to make sure the other had counted correctly.

"A great earthquake came, and everyone ran out of their houses, everyone but the priests, who had not finished counting their money. A great gap opened in the earth and the priests and all their money fell in, fell all the way to the center of the earth, where there is an underground river. The church was destroyed, but gradually the people in town raised enough money to build another. The priests and their money, however, were never found.

"But there is a serpent who knows where the money is, and he lives beside the gold and silver and the bones of the priests on the banks of the underground river. The serpent comes up to town once a year, on Holy Thursday, and only at midnight. He has one gold eye and one silver eye and few people see him, but he sees everything."

Sometimes after reciting this fable, my mother would tell me again the story of my birth and the dream she had before I breathed. "I was afraid," she said one night. "I thought it was a terrible omen, you given life with the help of a serpent." She sighed and tried to smile. "But later I thought it might be good fortune in a bad world."

One time my mother cried. This was after she said, "Your father gave me a disease and when I urinate, it hurts." She cried silently, as I would have, and her crying caused me to say, against my will, "Passion." She smiled, a quick, joyful smile, dried her eyes, and left the room. My father and sisters, staggering with sleep, returned with her. Rubbing his eyes, my father said, "You sure he spoke?" My mother nodded and repeated the word, looking at him as if she expected "passion" to set everything right. But my father merely patted my head as he would a dog's and said, "Will you speak again in another fifteen years?"

When my father and sisters had left the room, my mother said, "He doesn't believe me." She placed her hand on my head and dug her nails into my scalp until I flinched. Quickly, she removed her hand and looked at her fingers as if they had disobeyed her. "I'm sorry," she said.

She sat next to me and looked a long time into my eyes. "I'm sorry," she said again, and I knew this apology wasn't for the momentary pain she'd caused me but for giving away my secret. Forgiving her, I rubbed my knee against hers.

It was a month later that I returned home from Don Miguel's house with my shirt full of money. My room was dark, and when I went to sit on my bed, I noticed my mother. "José," she said, "I've been waiting here a long time."

I sat next to her. She must have seen the bulge in my shirt, but she didn't acknowledge it. "A mother knows things about her children that no one else knows," she said. "I know that you understand more than anyone suspects. And I know that you need your silence; it's what you have to make it all bearable. Everyone has something. Your aunt has her church and Bible group, and your father his politics and beer, and you have your silence." She smiled. "And I have you."

She gazed at me until I smiled too. "We know each other," she said.

I sat in the room with my father, the mayor, and Lieutenant Rubio as they celebrated Don Miguel's death. In time, I heard them plot three more murders, all of which I attended, standing in shadows.

When Lieutenant Rubio and his two soldiers went to kill Don Felix, the owner of a paint store, he didn't open the door. The soldiers broke it down, their rifles punching through it like paper. I heard shots puncture the night—shots quieter and quicker than thunder—and saw the two soldiers haul Don Felix into the van as if he were a drunk companion.

I waited until Lieutenant Rubio had left the house before I entered. There was broken glass on the floor, the shards mixed with playing cards. Doña Lorena, Don Felix's wife, was spread on a couch in the middle of the room. Blood was splattered on the couch and dribbled out of her mouth like a baby's spittle. I knew she was alive, however, because I could see her pulse beating in her throat.

Before long she opened her eyes. She looked at me, then glanced quickly to her left, and I knew where to look. She tried to speak, but I slipped past her. To see the top shelf of the cupboard, I had to stand on a chair. At the back, behind empty cereal boxes, I found three old paint cans stuffed with bills.

As I walked past Doña Lorena on my way out the door, she spoke very clearly: "You devil." I waited until her eyelids fell over her eyes like heavy clouds.

I kept the money, a stack that would have overwhelmed a bank clerk, in plastic bags that I picked up on the streets: pink bags from the bakery and blue bags from the woman who sold tomatoes in front of the market and yellow bags from Doña Patricia's pharmacy. I sorted my money in the bags: the tens in the pinks, the twenties in the blues, and the fifties in the yellows. I put the bags in the corner of my room and covered them with a blanket.

I began to leave ten- and twenty-quetzal bills in my mother's purse, sneaking them in when she was bathing or sleeping or cooking. She would come to my bed nights and sit beside me, our knees touching, and speak softly as trucks rumbled past the doorway and the house shook. "Thank you," she said one night. "I bought myself some soap today, three little heart-shaped soaps that smell like roses. I don't want to use them. It's nice just to look at them in the box and smell them. Of course one day I will use them, but I'll miss them."

Another night she said: "Your father is doomed. A person can live only so long sentencing people to death like God. God doesn't like that, and besides, people don't like it either. They won't touch us, though. They think that because I'm a woman, I'm harmless. And you, they think you're a fool." She laughed, a sort of triumphant laugh, and shook her head. "They think you're a fool."

She pulled from her *corte* a twenty-quetzal bill I'd given her and rubbed it between her fingers. "We'll be all right," she said.

Three nights later, five guerrillas entered our house with rifles. When they came, I was awake, but they pulled my father, mother, and sisters out of bed and stood us in our courtyard. The leader gave a short speech, then said he would take only my father. Trembling so violently his teeth chattered, my father broke toward the back fence, and in their haste to kill him, the guerrillas shot my mother in the neck.

My father died instantly, a half dozen bullets in his back, although my sisters kneeled in the dirt beside him and cried prayers in his ears. After the guerrillas left, the neighbors arrived to watch my mother die.

Wailing, the women crowded around her bed. I couldn't get near her and saw her only through a screen of skirts. She didn't say anything. A woman tried to hold her hand, but my mother kept moving both her hands to where the blood was flowing from her neck. She didn't seem to be in pain; her lips, though, were pursed, as if in anger over a betrayal.

When she was dead, the women left, and I sat next to my mother until the sun shot light through the window in front of us. Two men came to take away her body, but first they had to uncurl my fingers from her *corte*.

The guerrillas also killed Mayor Gualim, and they probably would have killed Lieutenant Rubio but, alerted, he had driven to the military base in Cobán. By the time he and thirty soldiers returned, the guerrillas were gone. Lieutenant Rubio questioned my sisters, and they told him that my father had charged the guerrillas, all five of them, trying to protect my mother and the rest of us, but they had gunned him down as he was strangling one and kicking another.

Lieutenant Rubio repeated the story around town, and it was all my father needed to become a hero. My mother was buried next to him, and the priest said three words about her: "She loved him."

When all the mourners had gone—even my sisters, who had clung to the cross above my father's grave as if it were an extension of his body—I sat beside my mother. I imagined her telling me stories, her voice as warm and soft as the rain that fell. I knew I could speak to her now, could tell her anything. But, as always, I didn't need to.

Three weeks later, my sister Florinda married Lieutenant Rubio. They slept in my mother and father's room, the entrance to which Lieutenant Rubio fortified by replacing the wood door with a metal one. "The guerrillas will need a tank to get me out of bed," he announced.

I turned sixteen, an occasion only my mother would have remembered.

One morning, I left money for Florinda in her skirt while she was bathing, and that night I heard her tell Lieutenant Rubio, "The strangest thing happened. I found twenty quetzales in my pocket." Lieutenant Rubio laughed and said, "A gift from God." The next morning, I did the same thing; and that afternoon, as she was washing clothes, Florinda mentioned it to Lieutenant Rubio. Lieutenant Rubio didn't laugh this time but said, "You either forgot or . . ."

He stopped, a worried look on his face, and Florinda asked, "What's wrong?"

"No, I was thinking . . . ," Lieutenant Rubio said.

"What?"

"It could be the guerrillas," Lieutenant Rubio said, and he explained that he'd heard that the guerrillas sometimes notified their future victims. It was a psychological game they played. A friend of his, another lieutenant, had received a cardboard heart anonymously every Sunday for six straight Sundays, and on the seventh Sunday a guerrilla shot him in the market as he was buying apples.

I didn't leave Florinda any more money.

At night I saw boys and girls my age standing out of reach of the streetlights, huddled in shadowed embraces, their arms so positioned as to make it hard to determine which arm was his and which hers. It was a game I played, divining which body part was whose, but this game, I knew, was only a pretense to project myself into the mind and heart of one of those mysterious, huddled figures. My thoughts on these occasions did not befit an idiot angel.

To have a girlfriend, I would have had to sacrifice my silence. In those unions in the shadows, I heard words and had no doubt that they were as important as the embraces and kisses. But my silence was my gold. So I walked down the long main street in town, peering into the shadows, and at the end of the street I sighed to the stars.

One night, though, I kept walking, past the *municipalidad* and park, past the uninhabited house decorated with political slogans from an election years earlier. I walked past the basketball court and down the hill, past the Caminos Rurales complex, where a dog barked at me before a woman called his name, and past the coffee fields, the plants looking in the moonlight like silver skirts. I walked all the way to San Cristóbal, where I knew, from listening at my father's meetings, that there was a whorehouse.

It was a wood building that used to be an elementary school. The word "Second" was still visible above one of the doors. A tall woman with hair on her chin greeted me at the gate and led me to a red-lighted room with three tables. A man sat at one table, slumped in his chair, eyes closed. Four beer bottles stood in front of him. I sat at another table.

"A beer or straight to business?" the woman asked.

I said nothing.

"A beer then," she said, and she brought me one.

I let the bottle sit in front of me like a candle.

A thin girl with small lips painted bright red stepped into the room and sat at my table. Although she wore a blue dress, she was *indígena*; I could tell by the way she spoke Spanish, flatly, as if she'd had to memorize the words: "I'm Dolores. I think you're cute. I haven't seen you before, have I? Don't you like your beer? Want to treat a girl? Yes?" She took the beer and had a sip. "Thank you. You're kind. How nice. You're cute. May I?" She took another sip, and another, and before long, the beer was finished.

"There aren't many people here, the day before market. Everyone's getting ready whatever it is they're going to sell. Tomorrow they'll have money. And they'll spend it."

She smiled. "You don't talk much. Don't like to talk? That's okay. That's fine. Another beer, or are you ready?" She smiled. "You're ready?"

She took my hand. She led me out of the red-lighted room,

into the courtyard, and then into a smaller room with a school desk, a chair, and a bed. I sat in the chair, she sat on the bed.

"Here," she said, tapping a place next to her. "Sit here."

I sat next to her.

"There," she said. "Much better." She kissed me on the cheek. Then on the lips. Then the cheek again. The lips again.

"What would you like?"

I said nothing.

"You don't talk, do you? Well, I'll talk."

And she talked a long time. I must have heard a thousand lies. Finally she said, "Well, what would you like? Anything?"

I pulled a fifty-quetzal bill from my trousers and handed it to her.

"Well, that's a lot," she said, "for nothing." She smiled. "But thank you."

I got up to leave. I had opened the door and stepped out when I turned back to her. The false brightness had drained from her face and she was eyeing the fifty-quetzal bill oddly, as if she didn't trust it. When she saw me looking at her, the brightness returned to her face, but I had seen her unguarded and she knew it.

The next night the three tables were occupied, so I stood in the corner. The tall woman with the hair on her chin brought me a beer and I handed it to the first woman who came up to me, although I didn't follow her to her room. I shook off another woman before Dolores approached me. "You again," she said, smiling her false smile. "Buy me a drink?"

She drank the beer and then took my hand and led me to her room.

I sat next to her on the bed.

"How are you tonight?" she asked, her smile resolute. "You liked it so much last night that you're back again? You sure must have had fun."

"Okay," she said, after a while. "Will you talk tonight? I'm really not used to talking so much."

"Well," she said after more silence, and I sensed her annoyance, despite her smile. "I told you most of what I have to tell last night. Of course," she said, almost in a whisper, "I don't remember all I told you." She kissed me on the cheek, the lips, the lips hard, and she pushed her tongue into my mouth and I let it slide between my teeth and flick against the insides of my cheeks.

"What?" she said, almost angry. "What do you want? Well? Come on, what is it?"

I handed her a fifty-quetzal bill and stood. Before leaving, I looked at her. She was ready. She was smiling.

"You pay well," she said. "Too much. You know, the rate is ten quetzales. But thank you."

I didn't leave just then. I wanted to see if I could outlast her smile.

"Come again tomorrow?" she said, and then her smile fell briefly, as if an unpleasant thought had struck her.

The next night I waited a long time at a table and I saw Dolores go with two men; I shook off every woman who approached me. The tall woman with the hair on her chin asked, "Don't you like the other girls?" It was almost morning when Dolores finally came to take my hand and lead me to her room.

"What?" she said, and there was no smile. "I feel sick, I'm sick of this. I've got this terrible mess inside of me." She grabbed a towel and pushed it under her dress and wiped. She threw the towel to the far side of the room.

"What is it? You come here to say nothing? Well, what do you want? This is too hard. Come on, let's do it."

She grabbed me and pushed me onto the bed and straddled me. "Come on, isn't this what you're here for? Isn't it?"

I nodded.

She smiled, not her false seductive smile but a smile of triumph. "You are?" she said. "You are. Well."

My mute admission seemed to stem her anger. She got off me and I sat up. "Well," she said again and kissed me on the mouth.

"Well?" she said. "If you'd like, we can do it."

I paid her fifty quetzales and left without looking at her.

I saw Dolores talking with the tall woman. Dolores was shaking her head. The tall woman walked up to me. "Wouldn't you like another girl tonight?" I waited. Dolores shrugged and came from behind the tall woman and took my hand. She let go of it as soon as we were out of the tall woman's sight.

She opened the door and walked into the room and sat on the bed, leaving me standing. "I'm tired of you," she said. "You're like a priest. Well, I don't go to church. I tell you honestly: I don't like you. I hate you even. You come here like some kind of angel. What are you? A freak?"

"Talk!" she shouted. "Talk, you devil!" She started crying. I sat down next to her.

"I was born dead," I said.

My response stopped her tears. She looked at me, her eyes open in fear or interest. I was startled at myself, and afraid. I paid her fifty quetzales and walked quickly into the night. I'd given myself up, surrendered my secret. I was distraught. But at the same time I felt exhilarated; my heart thumped, my lungs filled with the sweet scent of roses from a nearby trellis.

I thought about staying away. Dolores would forget I'd spoken, and I could reclaim my secret. But although I felt nervous— terrified of what my life would be with speech—I was excited, and I wanted to reveal everything, all I'd heard, seen, and done.

The next night I arrived early, and Dolores took my hand and led me to a room. We sat together on the bed. She said nothing, smiling.

"I was born dead," I said, and I told her about the dream my mother had before I breathed. "I understood I was different from everyone. I knew I had a kind of power. Because people believed I was an idiot, I heard what they said, saw what they did, as if I wasn't there."

I told her about my father's meetings and the people who'd been killed, about how, because I wasn't supposed to be alive, I felt no obligation to them, no obligation to God. "I could have warned them, I could have told them to run away, but instead I took their money."

She asked about the money, about how much I had. And what did I do with all the money? I explained that I didn't do much at all with it. "I give some to you," I said. "I used to give some to my mother."

After I explained the rest—about the guerrillas, about my mother's death—Dolores sighed, as if tiring of my story, and said, "I don't know much about God. But I remember hearing, well, we all hear, that God is love. And you say you don't obey God, but you did, kind of, didn't you? You did love her?"

I paid her and left, but not before crying, another secret lost.

I waited the next night until it was almost dawn. When Dolores still hadn't come, I walked out the door. The tall woman with the hair on her chin followed me.

"I wasn't lying," the woman said. "Dolores isn't here. She's dead." I stopped. "I couldn't tell you in there. All the men would hear." I stared hard at her. "It's true," she said. "She gave some man a disease and he didn't appreciate it, and he came last night, late, and shot her. He was very angry. You'd think these men would learn to expect certain dangers, but . . . well, I couldn't tell you in there. I mean, if the men found out a girl had a disease, well . . ." She must have read something in my face, or thought she did, because she continued gently, "I know you liked Dolores. But these things happen. It happened last year too, right around this time. It's not what you'd call unusual." She paused. "Anyway," she said, smiling, "I know you won't tell anyone. Dolores told me about you. You don't talk."

I walked back to town in the growing light. When I reached the park, I ascended the stairs of the raised platform and grabbed hold of the railing. I leaned my body over it, as I'd seen Mayor Gualim and other politicians do during their campaigns, and made as if to speak. A crowd gathered: women on their way to market carrying *mandarinas* and onions, men who'd been waiting for a bus in front of the *municipalidad*. It was as if they were anticipating another miracle. But I could only have delivered the opposite:

curses against the cruelty of it all, the pain. And they'd heard this before—heard it from their own mouths. There was no miracle in rage.

I waited until their curiosity gave way to the practical: the bus came, the market called. I watched them disperse, and then I left the platform. As I walked down the street to my room, listening to the babble coming from *tiendas,* I knew I would never speak again.

My silence was the only thing I could never lose.

Three days later, Lieutenant Rubio was shot dead in the market. He was buying apples. Florinda sobbed on the floor of her room, my two other sisters kneeling beside her. Later, after Florinda's tears had stopped, they all grew terrified, wondering if the guerrillas would come for us. But they must have known what my mother knew—that the guerrillas ignored women and imbeciles—because when night came, their fears gave way to exhaustion. Lying in Florinda's bed, holding on to each other, they slept.

I stayed up and watched the dawn, wondering if God had ever stopped the sun before it rose over the horizon, stopped it dead. And if so, had it risen on its own, a sun not meant to be born but somehow born? And if so, was the day still God's?

Snow

When she was seventeen, Saida could have married César, a tall boy with a flat face and thick hair. Because of his size, César was awkward; when he walked, his feet moved more swiftly than his body, so he was constantly behind himself. He was especially like this on the basketball court. Saida rarely played with him—*she* was the basketball player whereas he, like most boys, preferred *fútbol*—but on those occasions when she did, she was afraid of him, given the way he went after a bouncing ball, his feet darting toward it, then his body following, swinging wildly, like a drunk's. He crashed into fellow players regularly, and it was more often they who fell to the court. She herself collided with him once. She had grabbed a rebound and had it securely in her hands when his feet stopped in front of her but his body continued its forward motion, as if the tires of a car had stopped in place but the car's frame had continued on, flying off the wheels to wreak destruction. Saida lost the ball and her balance and fell into a puddle just over the end line, hurt and angry. But she couldn't scold César long or bitterly. He was like a child or a puppy, his awkwardness none of his fault, and immediately after she fell, he came to her, apologizing, wearing his big grin with big teeth, and handing her the ball as a token of his remorse.

César had no problem convincing her to become his *novia* and less in convincing her parents, who saw his physical awkwardness as innocence. César would, they decided, be a good boyfriend, loyal and attentive and, best of all, harmless. They were wrong on this last point, however. Behind the junior high school he filled Saida's face with kisses while exploring her chest with the groping intensity of someone searching for a light switch in a pitch-black room. After two weeks, he asked her to marry him. She asked for time to consider. In the meantime, he gave her a tape of a singer whose songs were very popular, jangling from radios in every *tienda* and house.

Saida liked the music, liked the guitars that ripped the air with whimsical fury, the drums that pulsed like amplified heartbeats. And at first she found the words appropriate, painful and playful pleas for love. But as she listened to the tape a second and third time, she noticed that the singer repeated certain lines in several songs; twice, for instance, he made reference to loving a woman from "her head to her toes," and no less than four times he compared being without love to drowning. She knew this was the vocabulary of popular music, not by any means unique to this singer, but she came to see the tape as a loop of the same simple sentiments, somehow representative of her tiny town, with its repetitious days, its empty and silent nights. She was ill one night not long after receiving the tape, and lying in bed she had the half-awake, half-asleep sensation of walking around town, forever passing the bakery, the pharmacy, the Catholic church, the Coys' house, and the *peluquería* in a languid treadmill.

To marry someone from Santa Cruz, she knew, would mean remaining in Santa Cruz forever, and Saida decided this was something she couldn't do. She had grown up listening to her mother tell stories about distant countries with wide streets and sky-touching towers. She would lie in her parents' bed as her father snored and would follow her mother's voice into fabulous houses with gold tables and across mountains with sugar-coated peaks. Saida's grandfather had been a sailor, working out of Puerto Barrios on the Caribbean coast, and he had passed on his tales to his daughter, who in turn told them to Saida. As Saida grew older, she discovered from newspapers and television that the world her mother had spoken of was mostly her grandfather's imagination, yet even knowing this, Saida felt drawn to its promise.

Saida was the oldest of Doña Ana's three girls. When Lorena and Alicia were born nine months apart four years after Saida, Doña Ana was too tired after the end of a day to tell stories, so Saida's sisters never heard them.

———

Lorena, with a quarter-sized freckle near the left corner of her lips, was the more unusual looking of Saida's sisters and the more careless when it came to men. Even after the family had converted to Evangelism, Lorena could be found in the town's Catholic church, not in the pews or confessionals but in the upper rooms, dusty alcoves flanking the belfry. It was here, at irregular intervals, that she met up with Jorge, a young policeman with a mustache. What happened amid the stored idols and ancient *candeleros* Lorena never told, but the entire town became aware of her trysts when, having woken from an unintended nap, Lorena and Jorge walked, wild haired, down the stairs and into a funeral. From that day forward, the town called Lorena "Church Bells," and people would have pinned a similar sobriquet on Jorge had his three-month shift in Santa Cruz not ended.

Despite her nickname, Lorena was married half a year later to Rudy, a man with an egg-shaped skull who worked in the town's paint store. People said the paint fumes had dulled his sense, in addition to his senses, and that he never would have married tainted Lorena had he been of clear head. This commentary was probably started by Lorena's half-dozen disappointed suitors, who would have painted themselves blue to have married Church Bells.

From age fifteen, Saida's younger sister, Alicia, worked part-time in the town's unisex *peluquería*, cutting hair with the same inattention she paid to her teeth, flush with silver fillings. Doña Victoria, the owner of the *peluquería*, would have fired Alicia, but she noticed that while the female customers raged about their ravaged hair, the men came back regularly, some only a week after their previous haircut.

There was no question that Alicia, despite her teeth, was attractive. Whereas her two sisters were slim—at least until Lorena began having babies—Alicia was on the heavy side. She was, however, not fat, merely full, her body pushing pleasantly against her clothes. She was not beautiful, as could have been said of Saida, but sensual, and this, combined with her talkativeness—a cheerful ease with any subject a man having his hair cut might bring up—drove men to stupid acts of passion. Doña Victoria had herself witnessed two fights in her *peluquería*, both between men with crew cuts waiting to have the next turn in Alicia's chair.

Alicia herself was a woman of passion, and she loved each of her customers, although she made an intelligent decision about the one she finally let sleep with her, a young man named Rayner who managed a coffee plantation outside of town. Rayner was noble enough to marry Alicia when she told him she was *embarazada*, and wealthy enough so that she would never have to work in the *peluquería* again.

Saida completed two years of college in Cobán, the city fifteen kilometers north of Santa Cruz, but she knew education wasn't the way out of town. The math teacher at the junior high school in Santa Cruz was college educated and made about as much money as a coffee picker. The title he bore, *licenciado*, could not hide the fact that his clothes were several years old. Instead of returning to college when classes began in January, Saida applied for a job at the Hotel Mundo.

The hotel was an anomaly, a piece of modernity dropped on the frontier of Santa Cruz, a faded town travelers hardly noticed on their way to larger points of interest. The hotel was a series of small houses, divided in quarters, each quarter containing a room with a bathroom and shower. The houses had been temporary homes to the French workers who came to build the electric dam a few kilometers up the road, and a Frenchman, one of the project's overseers, had stayed to convert the houses into the hotel. He also had erected a huge dining room and gardens in the center of the property. The hotel was magnificent when compared even to the nicer hotels in Cobán, and it drew foreign and native tourists as a convenient launching point to the Biotopo del Quetzal, a nature reserve fifty kilometers south, and the waterfalls and caves at Lanquín, a three-hour drive north.

Saida got a job as night desk clerk, keeping company with the moths that fluttered around the bulb above her desk. During her first two years as night clerk, she met only a few hotel guests, men and women interested mostly in insect repellent or an extra towel. She was, however, a spectator to curious happenings. One late night, a German woman counted the stars aloud while lying on her back in the field beside Saida's office. Another time, the hotel's lone guest—a man who in the logbook had listed his address as Rome and his occupation as artist—sleepwalked into a nearby forest and, as far as Saida knew, never returned.

One night during her third year, a pickup truck pulled into the driveway in front of the office. A bearded man stepped out and came up to the office window. Saida opened it, and the man put his hands on the counter. The man wanted a cup of coffee and said he would pay twice what the regular price was.

"The restaurant's closed," Saida said, although she knew she could probably get in. The cook usually forgot to lock the kitchen door on his way home.

The man sighed and tapped his fingers on the counter. "I have a long drive ahead of me and there's no place to buy coffee," he said. "I left Salamá very late, and I need to stay awake."

"There's El Dragón," Saida said. "It's a cantina in town."

The man shook his head. "I'm Evangelical," he said. "I don't go to cantinas."

Saida nodded. The man sighed again.

"Where are you driving?"

"To Playa Grande."

Saida knew Playa Grande was at least a four-hour drive beyond Lanquín. The man would be driving all night. She felt sorry for him. "Perhaps I can find you some coffee," she said.

"Thank you."

Saida left the office and walked across the driveway to the restaurant. She tramped through high grass around the building to the kitchen. The door was open. She entered and made a cup of coffee. When she returned, the man was standing as he had been, drumming his fingers on the counter. Saida handed him the coffee, and he thanked her.

"What are you going to do in Playa Grande?" Saida couldn't help asking.

"I make marimbas. A man in Playa Grande wanted five marimbas. I'm delivering them to him. He is paying me very well. He also wants to buy my truck."

"But you won't sell your truck to him?"

The man sipped his coffee. "Yes, I will. I'll make good money. I'll need it, because from Playa Grande I'm going to Mexico. And after Mexico, the United States."

"How?"

"I'll have to walk from Playa Grande to Mexico. There's no road. But it isn't far. Maybe thirty kilometers. And in Mexico I'll take a bus to the U.S. border. I hear it's a two-day ride. And then I'll cross the border *mojado*." The man laughed. "*Ojalá.*"

"Yes," Saida said, nodding. "*Ojalá.*" She'd heard about people who tried to enter the United States illegally. She admired their courage but shuddered at the hardship they faced: the long, expensive trip, the dangerous crossing. If they were caught, they were treated roughly by the border patrol, imprisoned even.

She wanted to ask the man if he was afraid, but he put his cup on the counter and said, "How much?"

Saida shook her head. "Nothing."

The man smiled. "Why nothing?" he asked. "You're probably a poor girl. And I'll be rich soon. So here." He pulled out his wallet and handed her two quetzales. In the restaurant, coffee was three quetzales, but Saida knew the man didn't realize it was an expensive restaurant, a fancy hotel.

Saida thanked him. The man said, "*De nada,*" and walked back to his truck.

For months afterward, Saida thought of the man. She tried to imagine where he might be. Had he succeeded in crossing the border into the United States? Some nights, she was certain he had, and she pictured him walking down wide, lighted streets. Other nights, she doubted he had, thought he'd been caught at the border. She imagined him returning one night without his truck, walking slow and stiff, his beard falling below his knees like with some biblical figure. To save him embarrassment, she would pretend not to recognize him and would bring him coffee before he asked.

Just as she thought she would be confined forever to a life of nights, Saida was promoted to the day clerk's job. Less than a year later, she became the manager, organizing the messy books at the end of every month. As manager she was also called upon to oversee the visits of large groups, the foreign doctors on their medical missions and the soda distributors from the capital holding their annual meeting. Because of her new position, she was convinced that she would meet someone—some tourist from the United States or Europe or some businessman from the capital—who would recognize her talents and invite her to take a job away from her town.

She was not surprised when, six months after she became manager, a man from the United States expressed approval for the way she had handled the visit of his group, composed of doctors, dentists, and nurses plus a separate entertainment faction whose members were mainly teenagers on summer break. People in the group all attended the same Evangelical church and had come to spread God's word as well as to hand out medicine and pull rotten teeth. The teenagers dressed up as clowns and did religious skits in the central parks of the towns they visited. The man, who was gray haired and had acquired an alarming sunburn during his visit, explained all this to Saida in broken Spanish and, when he couldn't think of the Spanish words, which was often, in English, which she mostly understood, having studied English for several years during her school days. He talked to her one night in the hotel's restaurant after everyone else had gone to bed. He was drinking beer, and he offered to buy her one. She refused and explained that in her church, drinking was prohibited. When he offered again, she had the waiter bring her a mineral water.

She was about halfway through her mineral water when the man said he might like to invite Saida to his country. He wasn't a doctor himself; he was actually the principal of the school that most of the teenagers in the group attended, but he thought she might make a good nurse or, as he put it, "medical assistant." He knew of several institutions that offered scholarships to promising candidates in this field, and he thought Saida would qualify.

By the time she had finished her mineral water and the man four beers, he was nodding and saying, yes, that she would make an excellent medical assistant and he would buy her a plane ticket to the United States the very next day. He would have the airline send the ticket to her at the hotel. Did that interest her? She nodded, gleaming.

Would she, he asked, like to see some photographs of his country? Yes, she said. The photographs were, he explained, in his room. Would she come to his room to look at them? Yes, she said, although with some apprehension.

She followed him to his room, in the house closest to the highway. He entered and she stood near the door. He rummaged in his suitcase and pulled out a small album. He sat on his bed and pounded a place next to him. Sit down, he told her. She did.

The photographs were of snow-capped mountains and children in bright, heavy coats and puffy pants. "This is called skiing," he explained, in English. "There is snow where I live. Have you ever seen snow?"

She shook her head. There was a picture of an older woman, gray haired and slightly wrinkled, and a picture of the man and woman together, the man's arm around the woman. "Who is the woman?" she asked.

"My sister," the man said. "My older sister."

After Saida had seen the last picture, the man said, "You are very pretty. How do you say pretty in Spanish?"

She told him. "Yes," he said, "you are *linda*. That's easy to remember. Linda is a woman's name." He put his hand in her hair, and as he drew it out, his fingers caught and this hurt, although Saida said nothing. He put his arm around her. "*Linda*," he said.

He pulled her to him and tried to kiss her lips. She stood and walked to the door. She said, "This is not good."

He said, "Oh, *linda*, why? Okay, we'll just talk. You sit on the bed again." After a pause, she did.

He told her about his school and its 260 students. Many of them were Christians, he said, but many used drugs and alcohol; he was worried about them. He would have liked for all of them to have come on this trip with him and the doctors, but this was not possible, and besides, only the holy could come. He put his hand in her hair again and kissed her cheek. "*Linda*," he said. Saida moved a little away from him on the bed, but he shifted himself so that he was just as close as before.

She talked, as best she could manage in her unpracticed English, about how she had been waiting for an opportunity to work in the United States. It was not, she said, that she did not like her town; it was a good town with good people. It was just that she thought she could do something more with herself. She longed, she said, for something more interesting, more challenging.

Saida started. The man had slumped against her shoulder. He was snoring. She stood and the man tumbled on the bed, not waking. Well, she thought, well. She noticed, resting on a table in a corner of the room, an assortment of clown masks, one with hideous orange hair jutting out the sides of a pale, bald crown.

The next morning, she saw the man ordering the teenagers onto a bus. She said, "Have a good trip," and he said, "Thank you, thank you," and looked at her as if he knew he should say more.

"You will remember me?" she asked. "I would like to work as a medical assistant in the United States."

"Yes," he said, "I will remember you."

She was doubtful. "Do you remember my name?" she asked.

"I do," he said, without conviction. She would not leave until he said her name.

"Yes," he said, before boarding the bus, "your name is Linda. God bless you, Linda."

Saida dreamed that the man would remember her, somehow; perhaps he would contact the hotel, ask her name. Perhaps he had sent the airplane tickets; perhaps they had gotten lost or stolen in the mail. When two months had gone by, she wrote him—the hotel had his address on file—but she never received an answer.

There were always tourists passing through, men with ripped jeans and three-day beards and women with greasy hair and pendulous earrings. The single male tourists, the ones, at any rate, who awoke from their traveler's stupor long enough to notice her, to notice anything except the hotel's price—which always surprised them (it was too expensive) but by the time they arrived it was usually late and they couldn't catch a bus to Cobán or San Cristóbal, where there were cheaper hotels—the tourists who noticed her often made a pass at her, promising, after all their wondrous words, little more than a warm embrace and horrible body odor, even after a shower, and she refused them all, always with a smile.

Saida decided she could live without love for a while; she even told herself this in encouraging, silent speeches when businessmen from the capital, their hair slicked back and glistening in the neon hotel lights, asked her to accompany them for drinks. Sometimes she did drink mineral water with them, but she refused their more explicit invitations.

She threw her love on a man on a motorcycle. He was the director of schools in the region, and every morning on his way to inspect some village school, he passed the hotel, tapping his horn and waving. She imagined one day stopping him, jumping on the back of his motorcycle, and the two of them driving off toward the capital. When one day a new clerk at the hotel told her that the man had a wife in Cobán and a mistress in San Cristóbal and God knew how many schoolteacher lovers in the villages—he was a handsome man, he said, something Saida hadn't even noticed beneath his helmet—her love fled like a sudden loss of faith.

———————

Her sisters worried about her intermittently, pausing in their baby-filled lives to ask about her love life. Love was something they professed to know a lot about—the mere fact of their nonvirginity made them, in their own eyes, experts—although their own love lives seemed to have died soon after their marriages. Their dialogue with their husbands was a stream of invective and tears, broken only occasionally by a flash of endearments. Between complaints about unwanted late-night attention, they praised married life as "natural."

In her effort to spice up her sister's life, Lorena invited the paint distributor who made bimonthly drop-offs at her husband's store to dinner. The distributor and Rudy talked about all-night runs through the Chiquimula desert as Lorena nursed her baby and Saida looked out the window, wondering what snow was like.

"You know, there are plenty of men still interested in you," Alicia said on another occasion, running off the names—Ramiro Aguilar, Felipe Güe, Augusto Morán, Donald Ordoñez, Carlos Escobar—until she yelped because her baby had bitten too hard on her breast.

Saida knew she was still attractive, perhaps more so now than ever, but she also knew she had acquired a reputation around town as haughty, righteous, and—in a conversation between men she overheard in the shadows outside her church one night—*loca*.

When she considered her life and how she might define it, she thought about basketball, the one activity that was as sweet today as it was years ago when the world was a more promising place. She was on a team in town and had become, by chance, its three-point specialist. In the season's opening game, she had taken a three-point shot and it had fallen through the rim without touching it. From that moment on, whenever the team needed a boost, her teammates encouraged her to take a three-point shot. To her surprise—she never had strong arms, and the shot was from six meters—she made more than she missed, although she never tried more than three a game. There was a risk to taking three-point shots; frequently they crashed off the backboard or flew over it entirely, this if they didn't come up short, which was even more embarrassing. There was, too, an audacity to taking a three-point shot, to have the confidence that one could, despite the odds, sink it. Her sisters and friends, Saida thought, had opted for shots closer to the basket, layups and push shots from inside the foul line. But she, who wanted more, had dribbled over half-court, stopped beyond the three-point stripe, and focused on the distant target, its mouth as small as a baby's.

———————

For a long time, perhaps since Saida became manager, Don Pascal, the French owner of the hotel, a bald man with a sunburned skull, had been paying her more than the traditional compliments a boss could be expected to pay employees. He called her an angel, a charmer, and on one occasion, a sorceress, and this after she had done what she did every month—told the Frenchman what he had cleared during the previous thirty days. He began dropping roses on her desk, and she would have thought this attention the harmless kindness of an old man had not one of her coworkers said, "Looks like Don Pascal's enamored of someone."

He was not an ugly man; no men of a certain age can be called ugly, considering that most of their contemporaries are truly ugly, rotting away in coffins. Saida found something appealing in his smile—one that gave him the oddly satisfying appearance of a grinning egg—and in his refusal to speak Spanish unless it was absolutely necessary. He spoke to her in French, and she thought part of the reason that he liked her so much, the reason he gave her the roses, was that more often than not she understood what he was saying, and she even responded, when she could, with the little French she knew, although he understood Spanish perfectly.

Don Pascal had an old wife and old children in France, all of whom found it beneath them to visit his hotel in a Third World country, although they wrote frequently and shipped him wine, which he paid exorbitant sums to extract from the customs office in the capital. He made an annual visit to France around Christmas, leaving the hotel in Saida's hands for a month. After his most recent visit, he had presented her with a tiny model of the Eiffel Tower enclosed in a glass bubble filled with water. When she shook it, snow fell.

She noticed that he was around the hotel more often. Before, in the afternoons, he would go to Cobán, where he drank coffee on the porch of a German café. Lately, however, he spent time in the main office behind the bar in the hotel's restaurant, where

Saida planned menus and room assignments for group visits. Often when she looked up from her work, she found him twirling a pen and looking at her with the wide-eyed but calm curiosity of an owl. "You've grown," he said one afternoon. "Matured, perhaps, is the better word. You're a woman."

When she stayed late, so did he. And he offered her rides to her house, eight hundred meters from the hotel. She did not like to walk at night anyway. The dirt road out of the hotel was frequently muddy and there were only a few streetlights, half of which had burned-out bulbs. In the car, she could smell him, a pleasant smell of leather and whiskey, although he wore no leather and she had never known him to drink whiskey. Perhaps it was just the way old Frenchmen smelled, she thought.

One night, before she stepped out of his car, he took her hand and kissed it. "You are marvelous," he said.

She didn't confide in anyone. Her sisters, she knew, would not have understood her interest in Don Pascal. She didn't know if she herself understood. She asked herself if she was in love and concluded she wasn't. She was merely, she decided, on the far end of a dream, like coming to the end of a rainbow.

Days later, she allowed Don Pascal to take her hand and lead her to an unoccupied room, where he undressed her in the comforting dimness of the twenty-five-watt bulbs about which so many guests complained. She waited for what seemed ages, accepting his kisses everywhere, before he was inside her. Afterward he apologized like a little boy who had stolen money from his mother. "I'm sorry. I had no idea you were a virgin." He slept as she stared at the white ceiling. Its paint, she noted, was peeling, small flakes threatening to fall.

They kept their relationship as covert as possible—he even stopped giving her roses, publicly at least—but the employees found out. No one said anything to her; no one was willing to risk their job on a joke in her presence. But she saw smiles she had not seen before. Word spread to town. Conversations ceased when she walked into *tiendas*.

One night after dinner, Lorena asked Saida to accompany her to her room. From a table beside the bed, Lorena picked up a pamphlet, which she handed to Saida. The pamphlet was titled "El

Adulterio: Un Pecado Grave," and inside it had a special section called "La Otra Mujer," which described the type of hell such a woman could expect.

"Read it carefully," Lorena said, nodding sadly.

A week later, Saida saw Alicia in front of a tomato vendor in the market. Alicia touched Saida's face and ran her fingers delicately over her cheeks and chin. "As smooth as always," she said. "Like this." She picked up a fresh tomato, its slick surface reflecting the neon lights overhead. Alicia dropped the new tomato and picked up a rotting one, its skin thick and wrinkled. "Not like this."

Saida couldn't say she was happy. She wondered, in fact, if happiness were merely some kind of confusion that happened to one sporadically in one's youth, a chance jumble of nerves and heartbeats, with the likelihood of recurrence diminishing over the years. She recognized, on the eve of her thirtieth birthday, something different in herself, however. She was calm, and her tranquillity allowed her a certain levity, a perch upon which to observe herself. She recognized that she liked certain things; she liked the glowing numbers on the calculator that showed the hotel's profits at the end of the month; she liked to hear businessmen from the capital drink their way into song; she liked the way the old Frenchman's hand curved around her stomach as he dozed. She liked these things and acknowledged with a smile that she hadn't sought them.

Just before the rains, Don Pascal received an express letter saying his wife was seriously ill. He told Saida he would be gone a few weeks, perhaps a month. She was to run the hotel as she did during his Christmas vacations. When he left the next morning for the capital, he waved and beeped his horn, just as the man on the motorcycle, the adulterous director of schools, had a few years before.

He did not write or call. She didn't expect him to. But after five weeks, she began to wonder if he was ever coming back. She wondered if he himself had become ill. Perhaps he had even died on the plane ride, although she hadn't heard about a plane crash. Perhaps he had simply decided to remain in France, his life in a distant country abandoned.

The hotel was making more money than ever. Saida's reputation as a superb planner of conferences had spread; the heads of visiting groups frequently told her how the hotel had been recommended to them. The hotel hosted Evangelical and Catholic groups within a week of each other, and Pepsi and Coca-Cola distributors exactly fourteen days apart.

The employees assumed she was in regular contact with the Frenchman, and she did nothing to discourage their impression. She made certain changes around the hotel as if he had ordered them. She bought three classical guitars with which the boisterous businessmen could accompany themselves at evening's end. She had seventy-five-watt bulbs installed in the rooms. She made English versions of the restaurant menu.

After stacking the hotel's profits in the small safe behind the bar for two months, she ran out of room. She went to Cobán and opened a bank account in her own name. This was the only way she knew to keep the hotel's money safe. When Don Pascal returned, she would turn the money over to him.

But Don Pascal did not return. He sent no letter. He did not call.

She had rosebushes planted beside the walkways between hotel rooms. She placed advertisements in travel magazines in the United States. She had a basketball court built behind the parking lot. The guests kept coming, even when she doubled the rates.

One morning, Saida stepped away from the bank counter and realized she had enough money to go anywhere in the world.

The rough rains had stopped, but there was still an occasional sprinkle, the area's famous *chipi-chipi*, and days were unusually cool—on certain days, people could even see their breath—but this was not sufficient reason to delay the start of the basketball season. Saida didn't know whether her skills had diminished in the last few years or whether the women she played against, some of them really only girls, had gotten better, but she found it harder to free herself for a shot. And the shots she did take were usually unfortunate efforts, landing wide or short of the rim. The team had a new three-point specialist, a girl from the junior high named Clarita who boldly fired up shots from anywhere inside the half-court line.

They were a good team, perhaps the league's best, although

most of the games were close. It was during such a close game that the clouds began to trickle in over the mountains like people into church. By the time the second half started, a cool wind, cold even, had kicked up. Saida's team was either winning by a little or losing by a little. There was no scoreboard; whoever had a pen kept score, sitting on the weed-dotted concrete base of an unfinished house beside the court.

Passing up a three-point shot, Clarita bounced a pass to Saida, who had been left uncovered. She stood a step outside the three-point stripe. She bounced the ball, caught it, decided to shoot. Then it began to rain, no, something harder than rain, something heavy and hard. The court cleared instantly, as if people were fleeing a fire. "What?" Saida said, and she saw Clarita waving at her. "Come on!" Clarita shouted.

Saida saw what was falling. Solid and white. Snow. This must be snow, she thought. It tapped her head. "It's snow!" Saida announced.

"It's ice!" Clarita shouted, her arms flung over her head. "Ice! Come on!"

Saida followed Clarita off the court. Laughing, she held the basketball above her head, protecting herself from whatever it was that was falling.

A
Detective's
Story

Ramiro Caal knew immediately why he'd been given the case. The boy was *indígena*, like him. Rather, the boy had been like him. Ramiro couldn't say they were the same now. The boy lay naked and curled as if sleeping on a hillside dotted with soda cans and plastic wrappers, one of the town's dump sites. Most of the trash had found its way to the bottom of the hill and into the river, but the boy had slid only halfway down. He had come to rest against a sack of rotting potatoes.

Ramiro would have to guess here and now exactly how the boy had died. There would be no autopsy. The government, even in a large town such as Antigua, had little money to spend on the living poor, much less the dead. Ramiro bent down, his nostrils filling with the stench of the hillside, and touched the boy. The last dead person he had touched was his grandmother, years before, when she lay in her coffin and he, a curious six-year-old who knew no better, opened the glass door above her face and ran a finger across her lips.

He looked for wounds but found none. He felt the boy's spine from the waist. It was firm until he reached the neck. He could flex the boy's head as if it were attached to the rest of his body by a string. He noticed that the boy's buttocks were covered with dirt, which no doubt had accumulated during his slide down the hillside. The rest of his body was as clean as a baby's.

The two men in the ambulance crew stood, impatient, at the top of the hill. They were waiting to take away the boy. One of the men said, "Can we collect the garbage now?"

Ramiro stared hard at him. From his look, Ramiro made it obvious that he did not like the man's joke, but this did not stop the man from smiling. "What's wrong, detective," he said, "was he a relative of yours?" The other man in the ambulance crew laughed. Ramiro was used to this kind of laughter from the two other detectives in his office, both older men, both *ladino*. It was a laughter he had grown comfortable with, despite its undertones. He smiled.

"We're all brothers," Ramiro said. "Or don't you believe in Christ?"

He walked up the hillside and past the two men. He picked his bicycle off the grass. His office had only two cars, and they were not his to use. He did not mind riding his bike today. He needed the jarring sensation of the wheels churning over the cobblestone streets. He needed to be awake. After two years as a detective, he had his first case.

Before coming to Antigua, Ramiro had been a court translator in Cobán, a large city in the north of the country, near his hometown of Santa Cruz. The job had required a college degree, which he had earned at the extension campus of the national university in Cobán. The work did not pay enough to enable him to move out of his parents' house, but he had been grateful for the job. He saw too many of his friends from town without steady work, waiting for the coffee harvest season or for an occasional job illegally cutting down trees for lumber mills.

He had been good at his job. His first language was Pokomchí, the local Maya language, but he had learned Spanish flawlessly while in school; and because he had no accent, no one could tell solely by his voice that he was *indígena*. He looked *indígena*, however, with dark skin and a square face with a nose that dominated it like a temple on a flat landscape.

The lawyers he worked with liked him, despite themselves. They were all *ladino*, and they all reminded him, in ways subtle and obvious, that he wasn't. They learned, however, to appreciate his talent. Not only could he move from Spanish to Pokomchí and vice versa with hardly a pause, but he made an effort, through both word and gesture, to translate the nuances that the lawyers injected into their presentations. The fact that Ramiro recognized the lawyers' subtlety—their irony and veiled disdain—made the lawyers think he admired them.

Although Ramiro may have recognized their subtlety, he thought it a waste of time, considering to whom it was directed. Most of the people who needed a translator were poor, illiterate farmers who were too unnerved by having to leave their villages in order to appear in court to recognize, much less respond to, any fine distinctions in language. Nevertheless, Ramiro enjoyed the challenge of finding the perfect translation, one that captured not only the words but the spirit of what was being said. On one occasion, a lawyer ended a question by using *noches* and *coches* in a couplet—the defendant had been accused of stealing a pig on three consecutive nights—and turned to Ramiro with grinning expectation. If he were to preserve the poetry, Ramiro could not translate the question literally, because the two words did not rhyme in Pokomchí. He therefore ended his translation with sentences ending in *ixim* (corn) and Elim (the name of the church the man attended). This had the unforeseen effect of making the man break into tears and confess his crime, an event the lawyer celebrated by slapping Ramiro on the back.

When Ramiro received the offer to become a detective in Antigua, he was as surprised as the lawyers. The letter he received said the government was looking to put indigenous people in more visible positions within certain powerful agencies in order to comply with a provision that accompanied the latest financial aid from the United States of America. The provision required the government "to increase substantially the number of indigenous people in positions where human rights abuses against indigenous people have been committed in the past, including the military and police." Ramiro was to become the third detective in Antigua, one of the country's most popular tourist sites because of its crumbling churches from the sixteenth and seventeenth centuries and its location beneath three serene volcanoes.

The lawyers threw him a good-bye party. They said he was the best man for the job. "And when you fail," said one lawyer soothingly, "you can come back here and translate again. We'll save your place." They drank to Ramiro's inevitable return.

Ramiro knew that the government was setting him up to fail, and he suspected he wasn't alone. He wondered how many *indígena* soldiers were now lieutenants, and how many would be stripped of their bars when it was "discovered" that they could not read. He wondered how quickly he would be sent back to Cobán, and the thought didn't shame him. He knew his return would lead to prolonged teasing from the lawyers, but at least he would be with his parents again. And he knew the lawyers would be true to their word: his job would be there when he returned. He would not have to pick coffee or chop down trees.

On the night of Ramiro's good-bye party, the lawyers drank themselves into slurred incomprehension and Ramiro allowed himself to picture success: a house in Antigua, a wife, and a string of cases that, with certain acts of determination and intelligence, he solved, to the amazement of everyone.

The man from the morgue called. The boy's mother had shown up, having looked everywhere else. Ramiro rode his bike to the morgue. The boy's mother was a large woman who spoke hardly any Spanish. In his two years in Antigua, Ramiro had learned a good deal of the local Maya language, Cakchiquel, but he wasn't fluent. Her conversation was a mournful stream, and to Ramiro it seemed even sadder because he was unfamiliar with several of the words she used. "I do not know, I do not know why he *kamik*. Why would someone *t'ajinik* him. He was a *nak'* boy. I want to *xa'onik*. He never *poqonanik* anyone. Such a good boy."

The boy's name was Mario, and he had just turned fifteen years old.

Ramiro asked the woman if he could come home with her in order to speak to her husband, and she gave her permission. She lived in Santa María de Jesús, a town at the base of Volcano Agua. Ramiro sat on a wood stool outside her house, watching the clouds slide across the volcano, and waited. Her husband was working in the fields. The woman brought Ramiro coffee. She did not stay to sit with him, however, but returned to the dark cave of her adobe house.

Her husband arrived with a hoe slung over his shoulder. Ramiro stepped away from the house, allowing the man his private mourning. After fifteen minutes, the man stepped outside. He had not cried, but he hung his head, scratching one bare foot with the toe of the other. Speaking slowly in rough Spanish, the man said he had no idea who would want to kill his son. It was true, he said, that his son had been spending more time lately in Antigua. He and a friend from town had found work, although the man did not know exactly what kind of work. He believed it had something to do with the tourists.

"He usually comes home at night," the man said. "Late. Mario said the tourists do not wake up until noon, and so they do not sleep when we sleep."

"Do you know the name of Mario's friend?" Ramiro asked.

The man thought for a while, then said, "Chepe. He lives on the other end of town."

Ramiro asked if the man had a photograph of his son that he could borrow. The man said he did and entered his house. It was the woman who returned with the photograph. "My husband is very tired," she said in Cakchiquel. "He worked all day in the fields and now he is tired. Here is the photograph."

It was a color photo of Mario standing in front of his house. "A tourist from the United States took this," the woman explained. "She was here to take pictures and she took one of Mario. We asked if she would send it to us and she did. It was very nice of her." Ramiro promised to return it.

"I don't understand," the woman said. "I don't understand why."

"I hope to find the person who killed your son," Ramiro said in Spanish. Realizing that the woman didn't understand, he tried to say the same sentence in Cakchiquel, but he couldn't remember the verb "to hope" and he stopped and smiled awkwardly. In Cakchiquel, he said good-bye.

Chepe's house was even smaller than Mario's. It was a one-room adobe house with a sloping dirt floor and pictures of Christ, cut out of magazines, stuck to the mud walls. Ramiro announced his presence, but no one responded. He walked out the back door. Behind the house was a cooking hut with a tin roof. A fire was burning inside. Ramiro approached and saw a woman working corn dough in her palms, smashing it into the shape of a tortilla, then placing it on her *comal*, which rested over the fire. It was hard to see through the smoke that filled the kitchen, and it took Ramiro a minute to notice that, in a shawl on her back, the woman carried a baby.

In Cakchiquel, he said, "Excuse me," but not loud enough to be heard over the crackling fire. He repeated himself louder, and the woman turned. She looked much older than she probably was. Her face was beginning to wrinkle. Her eyes had lost any shine they might once have had. Ramiro could tell this even in the darkness of the hut.

Ramiro apologized for interrupting her and told her who he was. "Is your son home?"

"Which son?" she asked.

"Chepe."

"No."

"Is he coming home soon?"

"I don't know."

"Doesn't he always come home?"

"Sometimes yes, sometimes no."

"Was he home yesterday?"

"No. He hasn't been home in three days."

The thought occurred to Ramiro that Chepe, too, was dead. "Aren't you worried?"

The woman stepped toward him, as if to look closely at his face, then stepped back and began pounding a lump of corn dough. "Yes," she said.

Ramiro had learned discipline from his father, a doctor who refused to move his practice to Cobán or even to spend most of his time in his office in Santa Cruz; instead, his father, who had paid for his medical studies in the capital by working at night as a waiter, would tour the villages around Santa Cruz on foot with a cloth bag Ramiro's mother had made for his medical equipment. "Better to be your own man," his father always told him, "even if it means being a poor man." Ramiro's father found more satisfaction in finding a cure than in earning money. The people he treated rarely had cash and often paid him with portions of their harvest.

As a boy, Ramiro often accompanied his father to villages and acted as his assistant, writing down his father's comments as he examined a patient. His father believed that a doctor should make no diagnosis without eliminating as many possibilities as he could. During an examination, usually conducted on the wobbling wood benches always found in the villages, his father might come across some symptom and he would announce this to Ramiro, who would write it down, along with the four, five, as many as ten diseases that his father suggested the symptom might be associated with. And then his father would come across something else, and Ramiro would write this down, along with the names of more diseases.

Ramiro recognized a certain laziness in himself that he knew his father would be ashamed of, and when he caught himself doing less than he knew he should, he thought of his father and his hundred diagnoses for a headache.

In the mirror above the sink in his room, Ramiro stared at his broad nose. He wondered if he looked like his father. He sat down on his bed, beneath the single bulb dangling from a wire on the ceiling. He picked up the pad of paper and pen next to him. At the top of the paper he wrote "Suspects" and beneath that "Chepe."

Chepe, he thought, putting down the pen. Chepe and the rest of the world.

Ramiro had kept his job in Antigua because he did not complain. Despite his title, he was no more than a secretary and odd-job man. He drew up records on all cases that came through the office, most of which were never solved or even investigated, and destroyed records when his two colleagues decided it was convenient to do so, as in some drug busts in which the offenders, usually American tourists or expatriates, paid a sufficient bribe. On several occasions, he visited the morgue in place of his colleagues, who, despite their gruff exteriors, found this excursion distasteful, especially when the body was of some *indígena* person whose death would often not warrant recording in a file. A sense of respect and futility kept Ramiro from coming too close to the bodies. He merely looked at their faces and noted their skin color to see if his colleagues' assumptions about their race had been correct.

Ramiro did not like his colleagues, but he didn't hate them either. He didn't scorn their pursuit of bribes. Both men had half a dozen children, and because of all the tourists, Antigua was an expensive town in which to live and raise a family. Ramiro himself had never been in a position to take a bribe, and he had no idea if, given the opportunity, he would accept or refuse, although he knew he would feel ashamed if he did accept, given his pride in being the first *indígena* person to hold such a high position. He felt, too, a responsibility to those who, through pressure on the government, had given him this opportunity. He had a vague but persistent notion that he would, at some point, make the people responsible for his promotion proud.

There had been one celebrated murder case during his two years in Antigua which he, not his colleagues, had been responsible for solving, although they received the credit. It was, in reality, a simple case, one any of the lawyers in Cobán could have solved even after a few beers, but prejudices often draw even the best-intentioned astray, and in this case they blinded his colleagues.

When the American owner of a coffee plantation just outside of Antigua was murdered, it caused a sensation. The story made both the front page of the daily newspaper and the weekly tabloid *La Extra*, which paid an impressive sum to the night guard at the morgue for permission to snap a picture of the dead foreigner. Ramiro's two colleagues were assigned to the case, but the boss in the capital made it known that if they did not find the murderer in forty-eight hours, he would replace them. This deadline naturally made his colleagues nervous, but after a brief investigation, they scoffed at the forty-eight hours. The murderer, they concluded, was the *indígena* manager of the American's plantation. It was the manager's knife, after all, that had been lodged in the American's belly when the detectives arrived on the scene. The manager's fingerprints were even on the knife. The manager was arrested.

Ramiro, who was present at the arrest, was struck by the manager's face as the police led him away. His face bore the resignation not of a guilty man, reconciled to his crime and punishment, but of a person who all his life had been abused because of who he was and not what he did. That evening, Ramiro read the coroner's report and noted that the knife wound in the stomach sliced downward; the knife had entered just above the belly button, plunging toward the anus.

Contrary to stereotype, the American was not a tall man, and the manager was. This fact alone should have made the detectives question the manager's guilt. The American had been killed at mid-day, presumably just after he had stepped out of his car, because the blood trail went from his driveway to the telephone in his kitchen, where the man had fallen. To have inflicted such a wound while the American was standing, the manager would have had to thrust the knife from waist-level with a downward motion, an awkward undertaking, as Ramiro discovered by practicing with a pen. Ramiro also considered the possibility that the manager had been bending down, or on his knees, when he killed the American, but he decided that this, too, was improbable.

It was more likely that a person far shorter than the manager had stabbed the American. Given that the only other person around the American that day was his wife, a stout woman barely five feet tall, Ramiro concluded that she was more likely the murderer.

Ramiro brought this theory to the attention of his colleagues the next morning. At first, they ignored it. "What'd you drink last night?" one asked him. The other laughed, considering the possibility of one gringo killing another absurd. But the logic of the argument was inescapable, and the two detectives finally decided to talk to the American's wife, "to kill your theory," as one of them put it.

They were almost too late. When they arrived, she was about to step into her car, which was full of her belongings.

She confessed tearfully, in bad Spanish. She had killed her husband in rage. He had had one too many affairs with the poor women who came seasonally to pick coffee on his plantation. He drank too much. And he wouldn't install a satellite dish to pick up U.S. TV stations.

She had found the knife in the manager's shed. Her fingerprints never appeared on it because she always wore gloves, even to bed, because, as she explained, "This is such a dirty country."

Ramiro carried two pictures with him, one of Mario and the other of Chepe, which Chepe's mother had given him. This picture had been taken by the same American woman who had taken the picture of Mario. Like Mario, Chepe was standing in front of his crumbling house. Chepe was a short boy with eyes buried deep in his skull.

Two days after the body was found, Ramiro walked around the neighborhood of the trash dump, inquiring at various houses if anyone had seen the boys in the photographs. The neighborhood, on the outskirts of town, was composed mainly of small concrete houses and an occasional one-room wood dwelling of the type that were more plentiful in the village where Mario and Chepe lived. Several of the people in the neighborhood did recognize Mario, but only as the boy whose body was found on the hill nearby. No one had seen anyone dump his body.

It was past lunch and Ramiro was hungry, but there was another house at the very end of the street in a cul-de-sac of pine trees. The house was wood, with mud filling gaps in the boards. He decided not to bother and turned around. He knew he was being lazy, however, and he cursed his willingness to submit to his laziness. His father would never leave a job unfinished, he thought. He turned around again and walked to the door. It was opened by a young woman in a *güipil,* a blouse whose red was more stunning than roses. She was obviously leaving. He apologized, then introduced himself. He held out the photographs and asked if she knew the boys. "No," she said, before looking at them. Then she did look at them, and he noticed a flick of surprise in her face before her eyes quickly looked away. If she had not known them, she would have looked at the photos longer, Ramiro knew. Photos were inherently interesting because of their relative rarity. "No," she said again.

"You sure?" he asked.

"Yes," she said, and she walked past him.

This time, he tried in Cakchiquel. *"Pach'q'onik?"* he asked, and her response was more pleasant, her voice lighter, more comfortable in her own language: "Yes, I'm sure."

That night, he looked in his Cakchiquel dictionary, and he found words to talk about his past, about following his father, the doctor, around to villages. This was how he would convince her to trust him. When after two hours he put the dictionary aside, he spoke words aloud in Cakchiquel. "I love you," he said, and in his bed, the lights off, he recited a whole romantic monologue, speaking, he thought, someone else's lines but delighted to be an impostor.

He called at her house just after noon the next day. She answered the door, and he handed her the flowers he had brought, six birds of paradise. He spoke in Cakchiquel, the words coming almost too quickly. She stood in the doorway as if guarding something, the flowers he had handed her part of her armor. But below the arch of a flower, he saw the girl's mother, a wrinkled woman with bright eyes, sitting at a table. He addressed her: "I have come to give your daughter these flowers and to say that my father was a doctor, and when I was young, I followed him to villages and helped him work."

The mother said, "Have some coffee," and the girl pulled the flowers close to her chest, allowing Ramiro just enough space to slip through the doorway.

Ramiro told the mother and her daughter the story about his father, as he had rehearsed it, and he felt the light in the mother's eyes cool, not with lack of interest but with comfort, like a room that is left dark because the company is familiar. The girl, whose name was Herlinda, said nothing, and when she left for work, Ramiro stayed for another coffee with her mother.

The flowers Ramiro brought the next day resting in her hands, Herlinda asked if he missed his home, and he said yes. He told her about the rain and how sometimes it rained for a week straight, and when the rain finally stopped he felt as if a friend had left and he did not feel right until he stood in the sun long enough for it to make him feel feverish. He did not tell her that he did not think often about home; to think about it would be to miss it and this would not help him. She said she had never been more than a half-hour walk from her home, and even then she missed it. Her father had died before she was born and her three older sisters had married, and all three of them lived with their families in town.

One of his colleagues saw him the next day in the market buying flowers, and he winked and said, "For your *amante*." By that afternoon, the other colleague had heard about the flowers, and he was not in a joking mood. He said, "Don't buy flowers when you're supposed to be working," and he handed Ramiro a stack of papers that he wanted Ramiro to file. Ramiro said, "The flowers are for the case."

"What case?" his colleague asked.

"The dead boy, Mario."

"You're still working on that?" he said. "He probably fell off his bike. His mother didn't have enough money for a funeral, so she threw him in the ravine. Forget that case. It's nothing. I must have been drunk when I assigned that case to you. Since when do you work on cases, anyway?"

Ramiro spent all day in the office, filing reports and typing letters to judges in the capital. On Sunday, when the office was closed, he went to see Herlinda. He had been reading himself to sleep at night from his Cakchiquel dictionary, and he even dreamed in Cakchiquel.

He arrived at her house just as she and her mother were sitting down to eat. They made a place for him, and her mother went to the kitchen and returned with a plate, the juice from the beans mixing with the fluffy scrambled eggs. Her mother had a cold and a sore throat, and when she was not complaining about this, she was silent. Herlinda did not talk either. Ramiro wanted to say something, but he had already told them the story about following his father around to villages. And he was not ready to speak the words of love he knew to Herlinda. They still seemed like borrowed words, although when he thought of them in his own language, in relation to her, they seemed genuine, as if he were not just speaking them but creating them.

When Herlinda got up to go to work, Ramiro followed her outside. He said he had not come the previous days because he had been working. "They make me do their work," he said, and his voice surprised him. It was angry, bitter. "They give me the title detective, and yet I'm a secretary. Except one day the two of them were drunk, and they got a report about this *indígena* boy being murdered, and they said, 'That's your case, we don't want it.' And it's my case now, but they want me to forget it, and they give me a lot of useless work to do."

Her head bowed, Herlinda said, "I know those boys you were asking about."

Herlinda worked in a tourist restaurant washing dishes. From the window in front of the sink, she said, she used to see the boys at the bar across the street. They stood outside at night and smoked cigarettes, then went inside, then returned outside. "They were always there, and then one night, there was a long, black car. A gray-haired man got out. Yes, he had gray hair, but he was bald at top, not very much but with a spot like a saucer. He got out of the long, black car and went into the bar. And the two boys went in. I've never seen the boys since then."

Ramiro asked her what else she remembered about the car, the man, the night. He walked with her all the way to the restaurant. She opened the back door. She said, "The man was a foreigner. I'm sure of it. Of course, in that bar, there are only foreigners."

The owner of the bar, Don Gerardo, was not a foreigner, but he dressed in imported clothes and had a self-important air that also seemed foreign. He did not like the fact that Ramiro Caal was standing in his bar.

"No, I've never seen them," he said, looking at the pictures of the boys. "Someone said they hung out here? Well, plenty of people hang out here. But not boys like these. Listen, this is basically a place for tourists. Tourists with money. Not for little Indians, okay?"

Don Gerardo seemed a little dazed, as if drunk or on drugs. "A gray-haired man in a long, black car? What else? The man is a little bald on top? Well, you couldn't be referring to the Interim Deputy United States Ambassador, could you?" He laughed. "He pays us a visit every once in a while. Of course, I must know a dozen guys who fit that description. And yes, some of them have limousines. That's the word you're looking for. Not 'long, black car' but limousine. Where are you from? Why don't you go back to your village."

Ramiro walked the neighborhood around the bar, asking the clerks in stores that sold native clothing, jade, and flavored popcorn if they had ever seen the boys. Some looked a long time at the photographs, but no one admitted to having seen them. Why should they? Ramiro thought. Why should anyone want to help? There's nothing in it for them but potential trouble. To become involved in anything out of the ordinary, even on the periphery of it, is dangerous.

He bought a newspaper from a boy on the corner. Staring up and down the street, he saw mostly white faces. Tourists. He had heard that foreigners now owned most of the land in town. People who had lived in Antigua for years but had always rented were forced to move away. Landlords wanted only U.S. dollars.

The newspaper boy handed him his change. Ramiro figured the boy was about fourteen years old. He asked, "How long have you been working here?"

The boy said, "Since nine o'clock."

"No, how many years?"

"Three years."

"Do you go to school?" Ramiro asked.

"No."

"Why not?"

"Because."

"Because why?"

"Because that's the way it is."

"Don't your mother and father want you to go to school?"

"I did go to school. I learned how to read and write. That's enough."

"Isn't it hard, working?" Ramiro asked. "Wouldn't you rather be in school?"

"It's not important," the boy said. "A lot of kids work. I sell newspapers. It's not so bad. Some girls sell jewelry and purses. Some boys watch cars. I know some boys who work with the tourists."

"What do you mean, 'work with the tourists'?"

"You know, doing what the tourists want. They work in the bars."

"What do they do?"

The boy looked away. "They make a lot of money. I make ten centavos for every paper I sell."

"What bars do they work in?"

"They work in the bars where the tourists are. A man asked me once if I wanted to work with him in the bar, but I knew about the bars and I said no. I sell newspapers. The tourists don't buy the newspaper much. They don't know how to read."

Ramiro showed the boy the photographs. He sensed that the boy knew Mario and Chepe; naturally the boy denied it, but he allowed, "Maybe they work with the tourists."

Ramiro carried the newspaper with him to the restaurant where Herlinda worked. He waited outside for her, reading under a streetlight. When she stepped outside, he swept her into shadows and they kissed. He would have liked to have kissed her until dawn, but his work compelled him to stop, pull out the newspaper, and show her the society page. "Is this man familiar?" he said, pointing to a photograph, barely visible in the faint streetlight.

She stared at it a moment. "That's him," she said, nodding. "That's the gray-haired man."

The picture was of the Interim Deputy U.S. Ambassador, posing between two candidates for princess of something, glitter in their hair.

The next morning, one of Ramiro's colleagues handed him a letter, which had been hand-delivered. It was from the boss in the capital and said, "Because of the inordinate amount of labor we are facing in the central office, your presence is required here as of the time you receive this."

When Ramiro got to the capital, a forty-five-minute bus ride away, he was shown a desk in a corner of an enormous room. After sitting an hour, he wandered to the center of the room, where a secretary had her desk, and asked if there was something he could do. "The boss sent for me personally," he said, with some satisfaction.

"There's nothing," she said. Then, as if to herself, "There's never anything."

In the afternoon, he was given another letter, signed by the boss, telling him that his work hours would be from eight in the morning to five in the evening, with an hour break for lunch. He spent the last two hours of his first day watching a spider build a web above him. Accustomed to the languid pace of government offices, he wasn't frustrated: he would use the slow time to think about the case.

He took the last bus back to Antigua. After making himself dinner, he read his Cakchiquel dictionary, which to him had become as exciting as a novel, the words promising adventure. At midnight, he went to the restaurant to meet Herlinda.

When she came out, she said, "Tonight I saw the boy you're looking for."

"Chepe?"

She nodded and explained that Chepe had come out of the bar, gone down the street half a block to buy something, then returned.

Ramiro waited three nights across the street from the bar before he saw Chepe. It was nightfall, but the streetlights had not yet been turned on. Chepe stepped out of the bar. He walked briskly up the street. Ramiro followed. Chepe entered a store and asked for a pack of cigarettes. Ramiro stood beside him, regarding the eyes buried deep in Chepe's face.

"Buenas noches," Ramiro said. Chepe returned the greeting. The woman behind the counter brought the pack of cigarettes and Chepe paid. The woman did not have change and went to look for it in another room.

"Your name's Chepe," Ramiro said.

"Right," Chepe said.

"I'm Ramiro."

"Okay."

"I'm a detective. I'm investigating the death of your friend Mario."

"I don't know anything," Chepe said.

Ramiro looked hard at him. The woman brought Chepe's change. Chepe walked outside. Ramiro followed.

"I'd like to ask you a few questions," Ramiro said.

Chepe repeated, "I don't know anything."

Ramiro switched to Cakchiquel: "Your mother is looking for you."

"Right," Chepe said in Spanish.

"She thinks you might be dead."

"I'm not," he answered in Cakchiquel.

"There's a problem," Ramiro said. "You see, many people have been looking for you. Police. They think you might have killed your friend. I don't think so myself, but a lot of people do."

"I didn't kill anyone," Chepe said.

They had stopped walking and were standing under a streetlight, now illuminated.

"I'd like to talk to you."

"Don Gerardo, the owner, he's waiting."

"This is important."

"He told me not to talk to anyone. He said I shouldn't even leave the bar. Then he forgets when his friends come and they go to the room in back. He sends me out for cigarettes."

"Come with me," Ramiro said, and took him by the shoulder. Chepe complied. Ramiro noticed that Chepe was crying.

They walked half a dozen blocks to the end of town and found two stools in the closed market and sat down.

"You know who killed your friend?"

"Yes."

"Who?"

"The gray man."

"Who is he?"

"I don't know. He's just the gray man."

Ramiro pulled a newspaper clipping from his pocket with the photograph of the Interim Deputy U.S. Ambassador.

"Is this him?" Ramiro asked. "Is this the gray man?"

Chepe nodded, crying. He said, "It was an accident."

"What do you mean?"

Some of the words in Cakchiquel were unfamiliar, but Ramiro thought he understood. Chepe and Mario were paid to have sex with people Don Gerardo, the bar owner, knew. The gray man liked to have sex with both of them at the same time. The gray man was rough. "He likes to pull hair," Chepe said. He pulled Mario's hair too hard and broke his neck.

"After that Don Gerardo wouldn't let me leave the bar," Chepe said. "I live in a room upstairs. I was afraid to leave." Looking around the dark market, he said, "I should go back."

"No," Ramiro said. "You should go home. Does Gerardo know where you live?"

"I don't know."

He took Chepe to Herlinda's house and introduced him to her mother, saying, "He needs to stay here for a while." Her mother brought them coffee, and a lick of steam curled off each cup. Chepe cried again. "I knew something was wrong, but the gray man wouldn't stop until he was finished."

Ramiro researched the case thoroughly, working at night, exhausted. Through Chepe, he met two other boys who worked at the bar, both *indígena* and from nearby villages. Like Chepe, they were reluctant to talk at first, but when Ramiro switched from Spanish to Cakchiquel, they gradually told him everything.

He knew Don Gerardo, the bar owner, could be convicted of running a prostitution ring. Convicting the Interim Deputy U.S. Ambassador might be difficult, but he thought this, too, could be done, if the right lawyer were assigned to the case (he knew two in Cobán who won without fail) and if he could convince the boss to have Mario's corpse dug up. Ramiro had read about rape cases in which semen was used to convict the rapists, and if Chepe were telling the truth, the deputy ambassador had left more than fingerprints as evidence.

Ramiro was not too exhausted, however, to meet Herlinda when she finished work at midnight. He would walk her home. And they would kiss for a long time in front of her house and exchange promises and compare dreams in a language that still seemed to him as strange and wonderful as the three volcanoes that stood guard over the town.

After three weeks, Ramiro decided he had enough information to present to the boss; his father, he thought, would have been pleased with his thoroughness. Stepping out of his room and into the starlight, he knew that he had accomplished something even the lawyers in Cobán, even his two associates in the office, could not fail to see as remarkable.

Walking to the restaurant where Herlinda worked, he permitted himself to envision the future. He imagined the boss naming him chief detective in the office. He imagined himself putting an end to the corruption and laziness; the office would be fair and thorough. No bribes, no uninvestigated cases. He envisioned Herlinda pregnant, her stomach growing each day along with his reputation.

He walked Herlinda to her door and the words left his mouth as naturally as a bird taking flight: "Marry me." Herlinda accepted and kissed him. They made plans in the moonlight: They would live in the house with her mother. Herlinda said she could not leave her mother and Ramiro said she would not need to.

———

On a Monday morning, Ramiro went to see the boss. He had never met the boss, never seen him, and he had to pass through a labyrinth of secretaries, each more inquisitive and obstinate than the previous, before he finally did.

The boss was not an old man, but he wasn't particularly young either. He was not heavy, but he wasn't exactly thin. He did not smoke—at least, there were no cigars or cigarettes on his desk or in his shirt pocket—but his desk contained a dozen ashtrays. Ramiro gazed at one ashtray with what looked like real hair, long and wavy, flowing from the empty oval shape in the center.

The boss said, "Sit down," but there was no chair for Ramiro to sit in. Ramiro waited for the boss to say something else, but a long silence followed. Ramiro said, "I have some important information." He had brought three folders full of notes; he handed them to the boss. The boss spent a long time reading them. When he finished, he said, "When did you have the time to, ah, compile this?"

Ramiro told him about working nights and weekends. The boss stared at him, and Ramiro wanted to see on the boss's face a look of pride, of satisfaction, a look he had been certain he would find when he'd thought about this moment in the weeks leading up to it. But what Ramiro noticed in the second before the boss broke into a false grin was a frown as profound and troubled as he had ever seen. He knew in that instant that he had done the wrong thing—for Mario, for Chepe, for himself. A smarter man, a less prideful man, would have gone directly to the Interim Deputy

U.S. Ambassador and said, "This is what I know about you. How much are you willing to pay so no one else knows?" He could have shared the money with the families of the boys. This, at least, would have been some compensation. Instead, he'd thought of the fame he would win, the admiration of men who would never admire him.

"I'll be in contact with you soon," the boss said, waving him toward the door.

Ramiro returned through the labyrinth of secretaries, who were more friendly toward him now that he had been admitted to see the boss. They allowed their eyes to rest briefly in his, and in their gazes Ramiro thought he detected a sense of camaraderie. They thought he was one of them.

Ramiro sat at his desk and waited until five o'clock, when a secretary handed him a letter. "Thanks to international encouragement," the letter said, "particularly from our benefactors up north, the government is making long strides in its effort to retire the foreign debt. The task remains formidable but not unconquerable. In its latest effort in this direction, the government is returning several public service employees to their former positions of service in the government. In the majority of cases, public servants will return to lower-paying jobs, but thankfully their valued input in the affairs of the nation will not be lost."

In a different print type, Ramiro read: "You will report to your former position as court translator in Cobán effective tomorrow morning at eight a.m." The letter was signed by the boss.

He thought of refusing to go. He could find other work, although he knew it wouldn't be as dignified as being a detective or even a court translator. The thought was fleeting. He would be risking his life by staying in Antigua, even if he never spoke a word about what he knew. The boss had been generous, in a way. As a reward for solving the case, Ramiro had been given the chance to stay alive. This was, he thought, laughing bitterly, something to celebrate.

Herlinda could not go with him. He knew she wouldn't be able to, but he had asked anyway, another effort at being thorough.

She had to take care of her mother, who could not live alone and was too attached to her house to live anywhere else. Herlinda promised Ramiro, whispering in the darkness outside of her house, that when her mother died, she would join him. They would marry.

He had shared with Herlinda more than he'd shared with anyone—his work, his frustrations, his love. For her, too, he should have been smarter, he should have thought twice before he allowed pride to lead him. But this chance, this life, was lost to him now, as she would soon be lost to him.

She gave him a last kiss before slipping back into her house and closing the door.

On the four-a.m. bus to Cobán, Ramiro was tired. He tried to sleep, but his head kept banging against the window. He sat up, surrendering. The bus was almost to Cobán. Clouds hovered above the mountains, as distant and amorphous as dreams.

Ramiro knew now: he was like those farmers in their torn pants and straw hats who periodically appeared in court, looking displaced and nervous. They were right, indisputably, and they could prove it. Their word was truth. But someone translated it wrong to the judge.

Ramiro did not stop thinking of Herlinda, even when he had fallen into his old routine as the master translator of poetic and passionate and polemic speeches before the court. He thought of her even as his own language returned to dominate his dreams. He thought of her, and he did not forget the verb in her language that comforted him when the birds warmed their voices in the morning and he still hadn't slept. He thought of her. *Oyob'enik.* To hope.

The Liar

When Carlos was eight years old, he went with his friend Rodrigo one afternoon to hunt deer in the mountains. There had been no deer sighted around the town of Santa Cruz for years, but it was every boy's fantasy to kill one. Carlos and Rodrigo had no rifles, so they armed themselves with slingshots. They spent two hours climbing a mountain just outside of town, which overlooked the highway that stretched from the capital to Cobán, the big town to the north. By the time they reached the top, they were tired and hungry. Neither had thought to bring food, but they knew they could cure their weariness by napping under the pine tree that stood on the top of the mountain like a soldier guarding the sky. They slept.

In the middle of a dream, Carlos awoke when he felt something tickle his nose. Two brown eyes were staring at him from above a long, narrow face. A deer! It was a female, thin and inquisitive. Carlos wanted to alert Rodrigo, who slept on the other side of the tree, but he couldn't speak. The deer licked his forehead and Carlos shivered with pleasure. "Rodrigo," he muttered, but Rodrigo did not stir. The deer kissed Carlos on the chin, then ambled down the mountain. "Rodrigo!" Carlos shouted, his breath restored. "I saw a deer! I saw a deer!"

Rodrigo awoke reluctantly. "A what? A deer? You did?" Rodrigo stood and stretched. He walked to one edge of the mountain, peering over it, then to the other. "I don't see a deer," he said. "You're a liar."

Carlos tried to tell him what had happened, but Rodrigo did not want to listen. "*Callate!*" Rodrigo said, and Carlos was silent.

Everything was silent. Silent and gray. The sun was like an orange cap on the head of a distant mountain.

"We've been here all night," Rodrigo said.

"How could we?" Carlos asked. "We just got here."

"Look at the sun."

"It's setting."

"In the east?"

"Well . . . it's a long way away. Maybe after a while the east is the west and the west is . . ."

"Come on."

"Your mother's going to be mad," Carlos said.

"Yours too."

"What are you going to tell her?"

"I'll make up a good story, no problem. What are you going to tell your mother?"

"The truth," Carlos said proudly.

"Are you crazy?"

Carlos did tell his mother the truth. His mother fixed her gaze on him. "There aren't any more deer in those mountains," she said. "You're a liar." When Carlos's father returned that evening and heard what Carlos had said, he shook his head. "You're a liar, a very bad liar," he muttered. He counseled his son about telling a good lie.

"If you're going to tell a lie, make it believable. Instead of saying you saw a deer, you should have said, let's see . . ." Carlos's father scratched the stubble on his chin. "You should have said you and Rodrigo went to take a walk in the mountains and you saw a blinding vision. And you couldn't see for hours and hours, and being blind, you couldn't move. But then someone dabbed water on your eyes. It could have been a farmer, but perhaps it was an angel, and you could see again. And then . . ."

Carlos did not listen too closely. He was too disappointed at not being believed.

When Carlos saw Rodrigo the next morning, he expected to swap stories of incredulous parents. But Rodrigo had told his parents a convincing tale about being abducted by an elderly couple from the United States who had hoped to turn him into dog food.

——— ══════

When Carlos was twelve years old, he met a young couple from the United States in the market in Santa Cruz. They were a pale sight amid the dark reds of tomatoes and the rich greens of peppers and the bright oranges of carrots.

Drawn to the inquisitive look on his face, the couple approached Carlos and asked him questions about his town. How many people live here? What do people do to make money? Does the town have electricity?

Carlos responded to each question earnestly and honestly, but after each of his answers the woman shook her head and corrected him. "No, it says here," she said, tapping a guidebook with her index finger, "that this town doesn't have any electricity at all." Carlos pointed to the electrical wires strung in the market, but the woman frowned, as if she had eaten a bad tomato, and looked at Carlos sternly. She said something in English to her husband, who shook his head and threw up his arms.

The husband said to Carlos, "We are tired of lies. We heard many lies in your capital and now you are telling more lies. My wife and I are tourists, but we are not dumb."

This wasn't exactly what he said, because he called his wife a husband. Carlos, however, did not point out the man's error.

When Carlos was sixteen years old, he had a tendency to keep to himself. He had few friends. He was not an athlete, so he did not spend the hours after school playing soccer as his classmates did. He liked to walk alone with a Bible cradled under his arm. He often walked beside the river that cut through town like a vein, tramping in the high, damp grass on the banks.

He did not know how to swim, so he could not partake of the river's pleasures the way other people in town did, drowning their heat in the cool rapids. He walked alone and listened to the music of the river, its roaring melodies.

He was walking on the banks, a hundred meters or so beyond a bridge, when he heard a splash and saw water leap into the sky. A small object was rolling down the river toward him. At first he thought that the object might be a bag of trash, but then he noticed it was a baby, as naked as the day it was born, kicking against the beat of the water.

Not only was Carlos unable to swim but he was terrified of the water. He knew this was why he walked on the riverbanks, to be so close to something he dreaded so much, like standing outside the cage of some giant, ferocious animal. He was not brave; he had decided this about himself long ago. Brave boys were the ones who performed daring feats on the soccer field, risking their heads by leaping high for towering passes. He was honest, not brave, and he could not swim. He was terrified of the water, yet he found himself suddenly up to his chin in the rushing rapids, stroking frantically toward the baby.

He coughed, spitting up water only to have it rush into his throat again. It seemed forever since he had left the banks. Finally, he captured the baby and held it aloft in his right hand as he kicked madly for shore.

Hours seemed to pass. His lungs filled with poison. But just as he thought he was about to die, he felt his feet strike something solid and he found himself standing in knee-deep water. He held the baby like a torch.

A woman and a man were standing on the riverbanks. From their clothes, Carlos could tell they were a poor *indígena* couple. The woman wore a faded *güipil* and the man had patches on his faded blue jeans, and even the patches were coming undone. Behind them was another man, dressed in a new shirt and slacks and wearing sunglasses that shot back the sun's fading light. The *indígena* couple were muttering their thanks, *"Intiox, intiox."* The baby was crying and kicking, but in Carlos's hands it felt as light and immobile as a cantaloupe. The woman moved toward him to take the baby. She said something to Carlos, but he didn't understand because he did not speak much Pokomchí, the local *indígena* language.

The man with the worn blue jeans spoke a little Spanish, and his words came out slow and broken. "We have a ride from Don Enrique. The pickup truck. But the road is bad. We hit and go bump. The baby leaves my wife's arms and flies like a bird. We do not know where it lands. *Gracias. Gracias.* You save our son."

Don Enrique, the man in the sunglasses, said, "Come on, everything's fine now." The *indígena* couple thanked Carlos again and walked up the hill past Don Enrique. Don Enrique turned to leave but then walked down the hill to Carlos.

"I owe you thanks," he said and sighed. He pulled his wallet from his pocket and handed Carlos a bill that Carlos had never seen before. The bill had a bright number 100 written across the middle.

Carlos was too tired to utter more than *"Gracias."* Don Enrique nodded somberly and walked swiftly up the hill. Carlos heard the pickup truck's engine rumble and tires catch in concrete. The roar of the truck grew increasingly fainter.

Carlos sat beside the riverbank, and the last rays of the sun were warm enough to dry his clothes. He walked home in the dark.

Gleefully, he told his mother what had happened. She frowned and began to cry. "Such a story," she said sadly. "Such a lie."

That night his mother went around town asking in the various shops if anyone was missing a one-hundred-quetzal bill. Don Pedro, the cantina owner, claimed he was, and Carlos's mother handed the bill to him with profuse apologies.

Later that night, Carlos's father sat with Carlos in the living room and whispered, "Son, you need to work on your lies. What have I always told you? They must be believable. If you had said you had met some tourists in the market and they had asked to hear the stories of the Mayas of Santa Cruz and you had told them about Mamamun and his doomed daughter and had frightened them with the part about the bloodthirsty *Guacamayos* and they had begged you to stop and had given you money to keep you silent, well, that would have been believable, understand? But this story about saving an *indígena* baby from the river . . . and you don't even know how to swim. Carlos, Carlos. Did I raise a son or a fool?"

Feeling more than misunderstood, Carlos cried himself to sleep.

When Carlos was twenty years old, he fell in love. This was not the first time he had fallen in love. He had loved a girl each year ever since he recognized the differences between boys and girls, but this was the first time his love was in any way reciprocated. Angélica was a short girl with long black hair and a round face. She came from a poor but respectable family on the far side of town. Her father used to rent land in nearby villages to grow tomatoes and peppers, but he usually grew what everyone else grew, and if he made any profit, it was very little. Eventually, a tomato harvest broke him. He had invested his entire savings in seed, fertilizer, and pesticide and his harvest had been robust. But everyone had planted tomatoes and everyone enjoyed a bountiful harvest. A pound of tomatoes sold for less than a square of chewing gum, and he could not repay his debts. Broke, Angélica's father was forced to work as a coffee picker on a nearby plantation.

Carlos's family was moderately prosperous. His father worked as an accountant at the Caminos Rurales complex in town and also taught math at the junior high school. Carlos was, therefore, despite his reputation as a liar, an attractive prospect for a girl like Angélica. And although Carlos was not very handsome—his hair was thin and mud colored and his nose was too long—and although he had a habit of keeping his eyes half-closed—when people did not call him "liar," they called him *dormilón*—Angélica told him she found him attractive.

Carlos's mother, recognizing Angélica's virtues and being even more aware that Carlos was not a very worthy candidate for an honest girl's affections, decided Carlos should marry Angélica.

Angélica called Carlos a liar the first night of their honeymoon. They were in a hotel in Lanquín, a town four hours north by bus that boasted caves and shimmering waterfalls. One section of the waterfalls contained a cave into which water poured. Carlos told Angélica about a story he'd read. During Holy Week, a drunk man had fallen into the cave and disappeared. Neither his body nor any remnants of him had ever been found. After listening to the story, Angélica expressed her doubts about its veracity by calling Carlos a liar. The accusation was meant in jest, yet Carlos felt stung. Even as he undressed his wife in the darkness of their hotel room later, he could not help but think of her remark. His heart sank, and he did not feel aroused by his wife. By the time he rid her accusation from his mind, she had fallen asleep, strings of her black hair rising and falling in front of her mouth in keeping with her breath.

The next morning, they went to the market in Lanquín, and Carlos purchased a watermelon. He handed the woman a large bill and she returned a few coins, not even half what he was due. Politely, he pointed out her error, but the woman insisted she was correct. Frustrated, Carlos yelled at the woman, berating her with a fury he found astonishing and a little frightening. His wife said in a soothing voice, "Carlos, I'm sure she's right. Don't lie." He looked at his wife as if she had stabbed him, but she stared at him with such righteous insistence that he turned his head.

He wanted to become his father's assistant at the Caminos Rurales complex, but the bosses decided he could not be trusted with the money and made him the manager of a road crew. He led the men to distant villages, and although the work had its satisfactions, being outdoors all day affected Carlos's health. Frequently he came down with colds. His skin burned easily from the hot sun.

And because his job took him to faraway locations, he was often away from home. His wife grew suspicious of his absences, accusing him of drinking and being with women. Carlos, who had never had a drink in his life and had never held more than a two-minute conversation with any woman save Angélica, was at first outraged by the accusations. His denials, however, only seemed to provoke Angélica, who began to describe, in rich detail, his various trysts and drinking bouts. "Tonight it was Sandra Pinto, wasn't it?" she said one evening, accosting him as he walked through the door. "I can tell by the way you're smiling." (He wasn't smiling, merely concentrating on holding in his bladder which, after the long ride back to town, was about to burst.) "She gave her measly breasts to you, didn't she? Offered them like strawberries. And you took them, you devil! You took them in your mouth. And then"—his wife's voice reached a feverish pitch that he imagined dogs in distant villages could hear—"she opened her legs and you didn't think of your wife, did you? You didn't consider your sacred vows, did you? You saw only the entrance to paradise and you walked right in, didn't you?"

"No!" he yelled.

"Liar!" she countered. "Liar, liar, liar!"

On another night, she looked up at him warily from the dining room table. "Been drinking again, haven't you?"

He shook his head.

"Liar!" she screamed. "I smell the whiskey all over you. What did you do, take a bath with it?"

As far as he could tell, he smelled only of his own sweat, and he pointed this out.

"Sweat?" she said, laughing. "So you sweat *Venado*? If you could only collect it like rainwater, you could sell it to all the *bolos* and be the richest man in town."

In succeeding encounters, his defense became far less energetic, although he always proclaimed his innocence. And after each episode, the word "liar," which his wife spoke like a violent benediction, fell on his head like a hammer.

Some evenings, Carlos would slip into the house prepared for his wife's outrage but find her silent and welcoming. She would have dinner ready, scrambled eggs and black beans, and they would eat together with the tranquillity of old friends. They would discuss the weather in such calm detail that Carlos found himself on several occasions close to tears, joyous at the placidity of their conversation. Rejoicing in the banality, he mistook peace for love, and during these lulls, he stared at his wife with an adoration most men reserve for their mothers.

These peaceful moments were infrequent, however, and Carlos aged quickly. By the time he was twenty-eight, he had streaks of gray in his hair. His face, exposed to too much sun and rain, had begun to wrinkle. He was even stooped like an old man.

In the town of Santa Cruz lived a woman named María Mo. She was an *indígena* woman who always wore the very finest *güipiles* and *cortes*. Her *güipiles* were dark red, and some had tiny white, yellow, green, and purple triangles, and some had small figures of men and deer. Her *cortes* were always dark blue, the traditional color of Santa Cruz, and hung to her toes. She was so well dressed that people called her Rabin Ajau, the *indígena* princess. They called her this in jest, however, because she was a poor woman who sold tortillas in the market. People figured she did not eat, instead spending all her money on the *güipiles* and *cortes*, which were twenty times more expensive than the used clothing imported from the United States that *ladinos* bought in Doña Alicia's Ropa Americana store.

The other notable fact about María Mo was that she was crazy. La Loca, they called her, even to her face. They called her this, perhaps, to shield her from deeper insults. They could easily have called her La Bruja, the witch, because she gathered unfamiliar herbs from the mountains and scraps of rotting food from the market and cooked them, the smell of her meals floating from her house and across town like a fragrant spirit. She liked, also, to walk around town at night, peeking into the cantina with her narrow face and bright eyes. The men in the cantina would laugh and say, "Get out of here, Loca," but afterward, their conversations would dissolve, and they would sit silently and would not even finish their beers before trudging home to their wives.

Children dreamed of her. They did not cry out in their sleep, as in nightmares; quite the opposite. They would often retire early, hoping to dream of La Loca, because in their dreams she would escort them to places they were forbidden to go, to the caves of Chitul, just outside of Santa Cruz, which people claimed led all the way to the city of Quetzaltenango on the other side of the country. In their dreams, they would follow La Loca into the caves and encounter collections of strange and magnificent creatures, which upon waking they could barely remember. But when they walked to school in the morning, they often saw shades of their dream creatures in the faces of the men and women of Santa Cruz.

One evening, an American missionary group preached in the Church of God in town. Earlier that day, the group's doctors had held clinics and prescribed vitamins and aspirin for the myriad illnesses the people of Santa Cruz paraded before them. The men and women of Santa Cruz professed enormous faith in the white strangers from the North, and although disappointed by the strangers' careless cures—the town doctor and the women who sold curative herbs in the market had more sophisticated solutions—they filled the church to listen to the American preacher.

Arriving early, the Americans took up the front three rows; the people of Santa Cruz crowded the back. The Americans had a video camera and were filming the people of the town, asking them, in barely intelligible Spanish, to smile. The people, as was custom when in front of cameras, sat grim faced, as if at a wake.

The preacher, a tall, blond man, began to read from his text. María Mo had been recruited to translate the preacher's words, although she was not known to speak English. No one in town spoke English. But because the visiting Americans spoke hardly any Spanish, no one could test María Mo's translation skills, and when the Americans had asked who could translate for them and she offered, the Americans had consented.

The American preacher spoke with fire in his voice about the serious matters of heaven and hell. After a few sentences, the American would pause and drink the bottled water he had brought from the United States. María Mo would "translate," and her translation was not the preacher's sermon but the legend of El Sombrerón, the dwarf with the enormous *sombrero* who wooed young girls with the sincerity and sweetness and sadness of his guitar playing. In the version María Mo told during the preacher's pauses, the dwarf played his guitar outside the hotel of a young American girl. The American girl did not hear him for the longest time because she wore a Walkman over her ears. She finally did hear him, however, and was impressed enough with his song to step outside to see who was singing. When she saw how short and dark skinned he was, she raced back inside. El Sombrerón continued to play, and the American girl felt sorry for him and returned with a handful of dollars from her purse. When the American girl handed the dollars to him, El Sombrerón stepped back, aghast. "I was not playing for you," he explained to the girl. "I was playing for the stars." The American girl, who did not understand him, thought he was asking for more money. She returned to her room, retrieved her purse and emptied it at his feet. Satisfied, she walked back into her hotel room and slammed the door.

Everyone in the congregation knew, of course, that María's words had nothing in common with the American's. They understood what the American was saying by his tone of voice and the occasional words in English he spoke that were similar to words in Spanish. Everyone, however, was delighted with María's story, and they laughed so loudly that the preacher stopped as he was nearing the end of his sermon to permit the laughter to roll over the church. The preacher smiled, too, wondering what he had said to make everyone laugh so much. He convinced himself that laughter had been the response he had intended to provoke— although he had been talking about the twin sins of infidelity and drunkenness—and he laughed along with everyone, wearing a big grin that could not, however, entirely hide his puzzlement.

Carlos was sitting toward the front of the church with his wife. He and Angélica were not Evangelicals but Catholics; nevertheless, they attended the sermon because everyone was attending. Like everyone, Carlos enjoyed María Mo's story, and when she finished, he laughed louder and longer than anyone else. When he stopped laughing, he noticed that María Mo's eyes were focused on his. He did not turn his gaze away, but permitted his eyes to rest in hers. He did not feel awkward or embarrassed. He stared into María Mo's eyes for a minute. His wife informed him that the sermon was over and people were leaving, but even then he did not turn away. He smiled at María Mo and she smiled back.

He could not sleep that night, and he left his wife, snoring through her nose, to walk in the moonlight. The streets were empty, devoid even of dogs, although he could hear them barking in distant parts of town.

He thought of his wife and the years they had spent together. They had been unable to have a child, and now they had stopped trying. His wife found comfort and fulfillment in her conversations with women who owned *tiendas,* talking with them below dangling bags of jalapeño chips and beside stacks of red and blue buckets. What satisfaction he found in life came from his work, despite the bitter heat and rough rain. Under his supervision, the roads were built quickly. The roads cut through mountains and made towns more accessible to neighboring villages. He saw *indígena* women, carrying baskets of vegetables atop their heads, walking on the roads he and his crew had built, and he felt satisfied because these women no longer had to take winding trails to market, although he wondered how long their bare feet would tolerate the gravel. (He knew, but did not like to acknowledge, that the roads were designed not for *indígena* vegetable sellers but for lumber companies expanding their operations into the villages' virgin forests.)

He did not speak about his work. He hardly spoke to anyone save for simple exchanges about the weather. Whenever he conversed for too long, someone always found some error in what he said and called him, with varying degrees of vehemence, "liar," and, as usual, he accepted their pronouncement with a gentle resignation, although he burned inside for someone who would understand him.

He was simply The Liar just as María Mo was La Loca and the dwarf of legend was El Sombrerón. The town had mapped out his destiny, and the harder he struggled against it, the more he seemed to fulfill it.

He thought about fleeing Santa Cruz, jumping on one of the busses that every hour beginning at two in the morning passed the intersection of the main road in town and the highway that led from Cobán to the capital. But on reflection, he decided his life wasn't as bad as he had made himself believe. He enjoyed peaceful moments alone and with his wife. And even if Angélica misunderstood him, she loved him, he felt certain of this, although if he had to gamble his life on his certainty, he might prefer another bet. Yes, he was misunderstood, but he was healthy. People had suffered worse than misunderstanding. And of course, he was right and they were wrong—all of them—and this distinction gave him a certain martyrlike satisfaction. They were the liars.

Outside his door, he thought of María Mo and her crazy, enchanting story. He would like to be the dwarf and play a guitar outside her house. But of course, he was no dwarf. He did not play the guitar.

Returning to his bed, he found comfort in the prospect of a long night's sleep. He awoke early, however, when his wife screamed in his ear. She spoke quickly and he could not understand her. He could tell, however, that she was furious. He tried to stand, but she grabbed him by the shoulders and pushed him on the bed. She slapped him twice across the face, and she drew back her fist as if to punch him in the nose, and he rolled over and covered the back of his head with his hands.

He heard her race out of the room. He left his bed groggily, wondering how he had managed to commit an awful crime during his dreams.

He put on clothes and brushed his hair before stepping outside his house. As far as he could see, the town was the same. The street was intact. All the buildings—the houses and the *tiendas* and the market—were standing. The sun was shining particularly brightly.

As he stood outside his house, his wife returned with a dozen women who wore angry, righteous expressions. They surrounded him, fencing him in like a pig. And they called him words fit only for a pig, and he listened, unsure still of his crime.

Finally, his voice shot above the barrage of words: "What have I done?"

His wife, arms on her hips, stared at him as a mother would a stupid child. "María Mo is pregnant. You're the father!"

Carlos laughed and said, "She's crazy," but the women's eyes narrowed and their expressions became more seethingly righteous.

Seeing that, as usual, no one believed him, Carlos clenched his teeth. "I'd like to know how she can make these accusations if I've never even spoken to her."

"You don't need to speak to make a baby," one of the women said.

"That's not what I meant," Carlos said.

"María said you seduced her again last night. And I couldn't sleep last night and I saw you walking around town like a dog," shouted another woman.

"That's all I was doing," Carlos pleaded. "I was walking. Can't a man walk around town at night?"

"I saw you stare at María Mo in church," another woman declared.

"I didn't touch her," Carlos said. "Her baby isn't mine."

"Liar!" a woman said.

"Liar!" another said.

His wife looked at him, and her expression contained mostly anger but also a sliver of pity. He almost loved her. She shook her head. "Liar," she whispered, and walked with the women up the street.

In the afternoon, his wife's brothers came to the house to pick up all her belongings. Angélica was moving in with her mother and father, whose economic situation had improved considerably since their daughter's wedding. Angélica's father was now renting land on which he had planted potatoes, just as nearly every farmer in Santa Cruz had done.

Carlos sat in his empty house. He thought of María Mo and wondered why she had chosen him to destroy. He hadn't done anything. He was innocent and yet always guilty. And finally he had lost everything.

He thought about drinking, but he was not a drinker. He had never been a drinker, and he couldn't exchange his good habits for bad even in the moment of his greatest despair. He was pathetically holy.

In succeeding weeks, Carlos worked with a mindless determination, pushing his ragged crew into the hours after dusk, leaving them thirsty and bitter. He returned home in a state that resembled death, his fatigue, once he sat down, freezing his bones so that he could not even stand to make himself a meal. Despite his exhaustion, he could not sleep easily. He often sat half-conscious in a stiff chair in what used to be the dining room (before his wife took away the table) until the sun broke merciful and warm and he rose for another day of work.

He had to eat, of course, but he had given up eating breakfast in the *comedor* in town, too mindful of the stares and whispered scorn of his fellow diners. He had to eat, so he bought bread in the bakery, mumbling his order with head bowed, and tomatoes and cheese in the market, but even these brief excursions left him vulnerable to the overheard remarks of the townspeople. "To cheat on his beautiful wife—and with La Loca—what a stupid man."

"And did you hear that he tried to claim he wasn't the father? What a liar."

"And La Loca is showing now. What is she, three months gone?"

"And he hasn't even spoken to her since the day he and she . . . What an irresponsible man."

His exhaustion haunted him, hunted him. At night in his stiff chair, he felt surrounded by accusing faces and he would scream out, his voice resounding off the walls and joining the other voices in his head. And yet when he was quiet and heard nothing, he imagined some presence behind him, some monster with a mouth large enough to devour him in a single swallow; but he was too tired to turn around, so he cowered in thought because he was too depleted to cower in reality.

One Sunday, off from work, his torment finally overcame his civility, and he rose from his stiff chair and staggered outside in order to face his accuser.

Two boys walking past laughed, and one said to the other, "He's drunk."

Carlos scowled, "I'm not drunk!"

The other boy said, "Liar!"

Carlos stumbled up the street and around the corner. María Mo lived in a two-room wood house on the border of town and the village of Chixajau. By the time Carlos reached her door, he could hardly stand. He knocked twice, and his knuckles stung as if he'd dunked them in scalding water. He leaned against the door, and when it opened, he fell onto the dirt floor.

He remembered nothing of the next several days, diving in and out of consciousness, except a smell sweeter than flowers and the sensation of himself delving into something wet and soft and his sleep afterward becoming less troubled.

When he finally awoke, after what he learned was almost three days, he was lying on María Mo's bed and she was sleeping beside him, naked and warm, breathing with the gentle ease of a light wind through cornfields. He was hungrier than he had ever been in his life, yet, tranquil and content, he did not want to move.

Gradually, however, he began to panic. He knew his presence in María Mo's house would condemn him forever in the town's view as a liar. He had proclaimed his innocence loudly and righteously, and if there were a soul around who still believed him — and he knew there must be, if it were a just world, there must be — then even that person's confidence would not sustain the bruising truth of his presence in María Mo's house. He sat up in bed. He, too, was completely naked, and he scanned the room wildly for his clothes. He saw only a few religious figures on the wall, pictures of Christ, crucifixes.

María Mo stirred beside him. He dreaded the prospect of her awakening. Softly, he stepped out of bed. The dirt floor was cold and dry. He looked under the bed but did not see his clothes. When he looked at María Mo again, he nearly jumped back, although her eyes, open wide, were not frightening, but rather warm and inviting.

"Where are you going?" she asked.

"Home," he said.

She laughed, a laugh part sardonic and part sympathetic. "Why?"

The question confused him. He did not answer for a long time, then managed, "Because."

To this she laughed, too.

"Where are my clothes?" he asked.

She stood, as unconcerned by her nakedness as if she were walking fully clothed to the market. He could not help but become excited by her. Her slim figure seemed both pathetic and desirable. She left the room and returned with the clothes, washed and neatly folded.

He dressed hurriedly, not looking at her. When he had tucked in his shirt and zipped up his pants, he allowed himself to glance at her. She was sitting down on the bed, her hands folded in her lap.

"You lied," he said.

She looked at him quizzically.

"You lied about me being the one who . . ."

She stared at him with pity.

"Well, you did," he said.

She explained patiently: "I have your child inside me now. If I didn't have it three months ago, does it matter? The seed was planted in the church when our eyes met, and now it has taken in my soil. It is growing now. I wasn't lying, only foretelling."

He looked at her, stunned. She smiled forgivingly.

Carlos went to his wife's door and begged entrance. Inside, he begged forgiveness. His wife's mother stared at him from in front of a door at the back of the house, behind which his wife was safely hidden. His wife's father sat with him on the couch in the living room and shook his head in sad wonder at Carlos's foolishness as Carlos's own father had done years before. Carlos never saw his wife. Permission to see her was refused, gently by her father, sternly by her mother. He walked into stiff sunlight and realized he had reached the end.

He returned to work the next day without the enthusiasm he had displayed previously. When the workers took more than an hour break for lunch, he did not complain, and after a week he joined them below pine trees, comfortable in the needles, as they drank warm soda and ate cold tortillas that their wives or mothers had packed. He even participated in their conversations, embellishing the mundane with bravado flourishes. They laughed with him and called him *vos*, a familiar term, instead of Don Carlos.

His house was still an empty and ghostly place, but he no longer felt its burden. He had finally reached what he was and he felt comfortable with it. He could even smile at himself as he stared in the mirror below the moth-covered light bulb in the courtyard and decided to put off shaving for another day. He slept well.

He didn't need the drink to return to her, but he decided to drink anyway, slipping into the cantina with the ease of a regular, plopping heavily into the wood chair, and calling out to the barmaid as if he saw her every night, "*Rosario, una cervecita, por favor.*" Rosario brought him the beer, and he drank deliciously, although he knew he would never have to drink again. He left too much money for Rosario on the table, and he felt glorious stepping into a street whose lights did not even faintly obscure the stars.

He smelled María Mo's house before he reached it. A luxurious scent emanated from her two rooms. Politely, he tapped at the door, but she did not appear. Instead, she called his name as if he had been invited, and he walked into her house and went into her kitchen and stood beside her as she stirred the soup.

The Whale

The river was moon colored and we swam, listen-
ing to the tremble of trucks on the bridge above us. You smelled
of sweat, the soccer sweat that still clung to you like cologne. You
were haunted because your last shot had caught in the wind and
sailed over the goal, over the fence behind the goal, over all the
people standing behind the fence, their mouths open in wonder,
and over the house behind the fence, where it disappeared.

You cursed yourself—your angry words swirled around the
packed stadium—but you were still great. Everyone, though in
tears, said you were great.

And that night we went to the river and swam.

Everyone said you went drinking in Cobán after the game.

They said you put your arms around a pair of women in rose-colored dresses and seduced them as they poured beer down your throat. You, who were born beside the sea, swallowed in great gulps, and the men listening at the other tables—tiny men whose wives were asleep in distant houses—thought they were in the presence of a whale.

You followed the women to a room and there made love with both, and you laughed like a great, roaring ocean. Yes, the men dreaming of love in the other room heard your laughter roaring through the walls and felt they were sitting beside the ocean.

But you were disconsolate, haunted by your wayward shot. Everyone said that, tired from soccer and women, disappointed and drunk on a hundred beers, you drove off the bridge.

No, I wanted to say and would have said if anyone would have listened. You parked your car and joined me in the moonlight. I had been waiting on the banks of the cool river, and you and I undressed. I first removed your T-shirt, uncovering your smooth, solid chest as you lifted your arms toward the moon, then your shoes and socks, caressing your delicate ankles, then your blue jeans and finally . . . but I couldn't tell them this. They wouldn't have understood, didn't understand. I would have said no and then told them about the whale.

But this isn't quite right, because I forgot the part they told about you sitting out almost the entire game with a sprained ankle and your team down by half a dozen goals. You could barely walk—the doctor said if you even tried you might injure yourself forever—but in the end you scorned weakness with a smile. The crowd roared approval as you leapt off the bench and ran into the game as if into the arms of a lover. You drove balls into the goal mouth: the first off your head from a distant corner; the third, from midfield, struck with such power that the goalie hadn't yet moved when it streaked past him; the fifth from just in front of the goal mouth, with your body parallel to the ground, as if you were swimming through air. You touched the ball with the very tip of your foot, but the impact was enough; it was plenty. The ball chewed through the back of the net like a shark.

You missed only your last shot. A tornado swept the ball into the sky.

You cursed yourself—your angry words swirled around the packed stadium—but you were great. Everyone, though in tears, said you were great.

Everyone said you went drinking in Cobán after the game. They said you put your arms around twenty women in rose-colored dresses—your arms as long and sinuous as a mountain trail—and seduced them as they poured beer down your throat. You, who grew up beside the sea, swallowed in great gulps, and the men listening at the other tables—tiny men whose wives were asleep in distant houses—thought they were in the presence of a whale.

You followed the twenty women to a bedroom and there made love to them all, and you laughed like a great, roaring ocean. Yes, the men dreaming of love in the other room heard your laughter roaring through the walls and felt they were sitting beside the ocean.

But you were disconsolate, haunted by your wayward shot. Everyone said that, tired from soccer and women, disappointed and drunk on a thousand beers, you drove off the bridge.

No, I wanted to say and would have said if anyone would have listened. You parked your car and joined me in the moonlight. I had been waiting on the banks of the cool, rushing river, and you and I undressed. I first removed your T-shirt, uncovering your smooth, solid chest as you lifted your arms toward the moon, then your shoes and socks, caressing your delicate ankles, then your blue jeans and finally your underwear, coaxing them down your trembling legs. Before we raced into the water, I kissed you, opened my mouth to accept you . . . but I couldn't tell them this. They wouldn't have understood, didn't understand. I would have said no and then told them about the whale that swallowed you.

How did they know? You weren't like Chepe, the man with bright white teeth who sat at the soda stand under yellow lights and grinned at every boy who passed, admiring the display of legs and ass. You weren't like Reginaldo, his lips as red as the tomatoes he farmed, who brought tired men from the fields to cantinas, drank more than they, but outlasted their sensibility with his desire and led them like lost children to his house at the end of a dark street.

How did they know? Away from you, but thinking of you, I covered my wife's body with kisses and drank deeply from her mouth, pulling from her lips the sweet remnants of her last mango or *mandarina*. Mornings, as the market came to life with chicken cries and children's feet pattering across crushed fruits, she spoke wearily of my hunger to the *señoras* selling avocados, and together they mourned women's fate adrift on the sea of men's lust. And you were simply the town's greatest soccer player, and your dances on grass drew delighted cries from men whose childhood fantasies you performed and from women who adored the sleek look of your black hair tinged with sweat and sunlight.

How did they know? We sat at different ends of the church, apparent strangers in that vast and gray space, I with my wife and you with admiring boys and men whom I marked jealously, wondering if they wanted from you what I wanted. The priest, whose eyes always rested on Doña María and her large breasts free of bras, said sex between men was the worst of sins, and you and I repeated "Amen," although I never meant it.

You tried, several times, to break from me, but even as you recited biblical passages to show me how wrong we were, your eyes devoured my body, tracing the arms and legs and lips that your conscience told you should never be yours again but which your heart would soon demand. And your excuse, the way you eased yourself back into my arms, was that your talent would blind them, would always lead them, even if they had suspicions about what you did with me, to judge you for who you were in your soul—the greatest soccer player our town had ever known—as if the content of your soul could be summed up with objects: a ball, a pair of cleats, a grassy field.

They had known about your great talent even before you came from the sea. Your reputation, it seemed, had been carried by birds or winds, because when you arrived at age sixteen from Puerto

Barrios with your mother, schoolchildren had for weeks recited your legends and old men had drunk themselves silly toasting you in crowded cantinas.

When you finally did bless their grass with your polished black cleats and your jersey loose enough to permit the wind to fill it like a sail, you defied even their dreams. Your miracles, conjured with the flurry of your feet, became commonplace. Balls you kicked vanished into sky only to reappear at the back of nets like curious-shaped fish swept from the waters of heaven.

They expected nothing less than a miracle from you when our town played San Cristóbal in the annual re-creation of the ancient Maya wars. The *indígena* tribes in our mountains had been more vicious toward each other than the Spanish had ever been to them, and those passions were born again in the thousands who filled Estadio Verapaz.

After your shot—the shot that would again have reaffirmed their faith—flew over the net, they called you *"joto"* and *"hueco."* They shouted without the tame bravado used for visiting players, whom they bombarded with similar epithets, but with righteous anger aimed at a brother who had betrayed them and would never be forgiven.

"Joto!" *"Hueco!"* They couldn't have been crueler had they lifted rifles and shot you on the spot. Their knowledge of your secret, amplified by their thousand voices, was its own barrage of bullets.

They knew.

After the game, you and I drove to the cantina on the far side of Cobán. The pretty women in the cantina must have known about us all along because they did not grin or coo when I did not wear the wig and long shirt you had always asked me to wear. (They must have been surprised at my hair, however, after seeing me in the wig. My luminous eyes and smooth face were like a woman's, but my hair was thin and sparse.) They said nothing when you and I left the table after our fifth or sixth beer and went to our usual room, and you undressed me in the dark, without your usual thirst but with an anger that made me want to cry.

You had always talked, in moments after love, lying on that sweat-smelling mattress that drooped atop the worn springs, about swimming with me naked in the river, as daring lovers in town did. You had left the sea but had transported its legends. Drunk on beer, satiated from love, you had spoken of a whale that would swallow us during our swim and give us its belly for our home.

Everyone, feeling repentant because of your death, forgot their words—"joto" and "hueco"—flung at you in disappointment at their own failed dreams and created the myth of your last moments. In their myth, they left me out of your car, and those who felt compelled to explain my bruised presence beside your lifeless body on the banks of the river said you must have driven into me as I stood on the bridge—I, not even worthy of their hatred, reduced in their telling to the role of a bystander at your great death.

But if they can tell how you didn't die and make it truth, I can tell how you didn't die and make it truth.

The river was moon colored and we swam, listening to the tremble of trucks on the bridge above us. You smelled of sweat, the soccer sweat that still clung to you like cologne.

You stood, waist deep, in the river. Your chest, broad and smooth, glowed golden. Your long hair held drops of silver water. You called me. I came. You kissed me, held me, my face pressed against your neck. I felt your heart thump against my chest, gentle punches. You laughed, not your boisterous laugh, polished in front of cantina girls, but a laugh you had never laughed before, a laugh of pure joy.

Holding me still in your giant arms, you said you saw a whale swimming toward us.

I said, "You're lying."

You said, "I'm not lying."

I said, "Then it's true?"

You said, "It's true."

And the whale came and swallowed us.

It was warm inside the whale, warm and as spacious as a mansion. I saw you slide down the whale's tongue and through an arch of seaweed, the entrance to his belly. You called my name, with longing and lust and laughter. You called my name, and your voice echoed along the walls of the whale's mouth, but before I could follow, the whale spit me back into the moonlight.

How They Healed

Armando Sierra and Maribel Biert married when they were seventeen, and their first year as husband and wife was consumed with daring exploration of the passion that had filled them ever since they met in junior high, Maribel having just arrived with her family from the Caribbean coast. But after the frontiers of passion were explored and mapped, Armando and Maribel were left with the task of governing this territory, and it was awkward because they did not know each other. They made attempts at conversation, as Armando tried to understand his wife's tender past. Maribel had grown up wandering with her father, stepmother and three half brothers from one town to the next. Her father was a soccer player, but not brilliant enough to be retained by any one team. He was constantly moving on as younger players moved up. Finally he quit the game, but his wandering became a habit, and he sought new jobs even though the old ones—as a bottler in a Pepsi plant, a bouncer at a topless bar, an inspector at a tuna cannery—paid him enough to support his family.

Armando concluded that Maribel probably had been drawn less to his looks—he was too thin to be called handsome—than to the stability he represented: Armando's family had lived in Santa Cruz for more than five generations, and he said he would rather die than move even the fifteen kilometers to Cobán, the big town to the north.

Despite the silences that grew more pronounced, more awkward, each day, Armando loved his wife. Lying next to her in their bed, he marveled at her breathing, a sweet whistle, and how warm she was, her body like a stove.

Three daughters were born, interrupting the silences. Armando knew, however, that his wife did not share his joy in the children. She often seemed irritated with them, as if they were hindering her, although from what Armando didn't know; on other occasions, however, he saw her be gentle with them, particularly with Karla, the oldest, who had her mother's thick black hair that captured any light and radiated it more intensely, as if their hair had a special energy converter. Maribel could be good with Karla, bringing her into the kitchen to teach her to cook, although she could turn cold quickly, too. Several times Armando heard Karla cry after Maribel had slapped her over some shortcoming.

Even before their marriage, Maribel had talked about going to the United States. This had been her father's dream. He had even attempted it once but had been caught at the border and treated so roughly that he never tried it again. As the girls grew, Maribel's desire to leave became stronger, and at least once a week she would talk about it with her husband. Armando at first dismissed her interest in living elsewhere as a sort of tribute to her father. But as the years passed, her desire grew more fervid, and Armando was forced to plead with her. He needed her, he said. The girls needed her.

But Maribel devised excellent reasons why she should go. She pointed out how little money Armando was making in his job at the electrical dam above San Cristóbal, a nearby town, and said that if he hoped to send their daughters—or even just Karla, who was eleven years old already—to college, he had to earn more. She said it would be only temporary. She would spend a year, perhaps a year and a half, no more, in the United States and return home with enough money to send their daughter to college and perhaps to buy themselves a car.

Armando liked the idea of the car, and he liked even more the idea of sending Karla to college. He had wanted a son, but Karla had proved even more delightful than he imagined a son could be. He wanted his daughter to have the best life possible, and he knew she would be freer to find happiness if she were educated. Still, he abhorred the idea of his wife leaving, and he argued against it, but not as fervently as he had in the past. Like his wife, he had heard of the fortune that could be made in the United States with just a little work. People *did* return from the United States with enough money to buy cars.

After listening to his wife plead every day for a month, he gave up. "You're right," he said. "Earn some dollars and come home. I love you."

The next morning, she was gone.

Luki Cul met Marcos at the zoo in the capital, where Luki often passed the time during breaks from studying to become a home economics teacher.

Marcos looked dashing and professional in his gray and orange uniform—so dashing and professional that Luki assumed he was the zoo's director, an impression Marcos did nothing to refute and even confirmed when he talked of "the boys" who worked "for" him. It did not strike Luki as odd that she would often find Marcos covered in animal excrement; she believed he was one of those peculiar professionals who preferred a hands-on approach to their jobs, like the agronomist she knew in Santa Cruz who insisted on actually planting corn with farmers instead of merely telling them how much space to put between rows.

When Luki sent a telegram to her parents to inform them that she was getting married to the director of the national zoo, they drove to the capital to meet Marcos. Luki greeted them at the zoo entrance and brought them to her fiancé, who was waist-deep in a pit he was digging, his eyebrows and hair flecked with dirt. A dead monkey lay beside the pit. Marcos quickly shook his head free of dirt, stepped out of the pit, and offered his hand to Luki's father, who shook it reluctantly. There was an awkward silence, which Luki's father broke by saying, "So you're a keeper, are you?"

Luki blushed and told her father that, no, Marcos was the director of the zoo. Then why, Luki's father asked his daughter, is he the one burying the monkey? Luki began to speak, but Marcos broke in to say that he had a scientific interest in the monkey. He had already taken a half-dozen blood and tissue samples to explore the cause of death and was burying it himself in order to . . . Luki's father allowed Marcos to continue for several minutes before interrupting to suggest that he bury himself along with the monkey. "Because a grave," he said, "is the only honorable place for a liar like yourself."

On the drive back to Santa Cruz, Luki's father told her how he had learned about Marcos. Suspicious of his daughter's good fortune, he had called the zoo that morning and asked to speak to the director. The answering voice, however, was female. "And of course I assumed the secretary had merely passed me along to another secretary," Luki's father said, "and so I said, with some impatience, 'Señorita,' and I laid special emphasis, and just a little scorn, on that word, 'Señorita, I am waiting to talk with the director.' Well, the señorita was the director."

Luki cried all the way to Santa Cruz, but there were two parts to her crying. The first was because Marcos had lied to her and she had been foolish enough to believe him. The second was because her father was an insensitive brute who had always ruled her life, and she could never live the way she wanted as long as her father was alive. Arriving home, she decided that, despite all Marcos had done, she loved him still, and more than that, she would never again surrender to her father's will.

. Two days later, Luki slipped out of the house at two in the morning and caught the bus to the capital. On the afternoon of the same day, Luki and Marcos were married by a lawyer who smoked a cigar throughout the two-minute ceremony, then, before pronouncing them legally married, cleared his throat and tried valiantly to shoot his spit at a nearby trash bucket. It missed, however, missed by a good five feet. It was not, Luki decided, a good omen. And she was already homesick.

After their wedding, Marcos and Luki moved into his small room, which he shared with another keeper, who worked the evening shift. Because their shifts were eight hours long, there was an overlap of eight hours in which they both might be found in the apartment, although as Marcos said without the slightest bashfulness, "I'm usually out drinking."

The first night, Luki finally drifted off to sleep at midnight but was woken when she felt herself being gently nudged to the edge of the bed. Sitting up, she noticed in the faint light that another man had climbed into bed next to her husband. She screamed.

Marcos awoke reluctantly, and as Luki pointed hysterically to the slumbering figure beside him, said, "That's Adolfo, the other keeper. There's only one bed. Try to sleep."

Luki couldn't sleep. She got out of bed and decided to make coffee; there was, however, no water. Even if there had been water, there was no stove. On the room's only table, there was a rotten apple and a pack of cigarettes. Luki didn't smoke, but with nothing else to do, she opened the pack. Inside was a deck of playing cards with pictures of naked girls on the back. Marcos, who had awoken, winked at her and said, "Adolfo thought I should hide them, out of respect." He then rolled over and fell asleep again.

She was unable to sleep on the edge of the bed. There was just no room. A week into her marriage, Luki had slept no more than four hours, but misfortune saved her. Drinking on his night shift, Adolfo fell into the alligator exhibit. Before he could escape, the alligator bit off his arm. Adolfo spent two weeks in the hospital, during which time Luki slept like a baby, having a luxurious half of the bed to herself. She was disappointed when Adolfo returned, but the missing arm afforded just enough extra space to enable her to sleep.

But Luki's and her husband's fate were tied to Adolfo's. Because Adolfo was missing an arm, the zoo's board of directors decided that he could be only half as productive and therefore halved his salary. Unable to meet his rent, Adolfo moved out of the room and back to his parents' house.

Marcos could not pay the entire rent himself out of his salary, and Luki's father had stopped supporting his daughter when she eloped. After frantically and unsuccessfully searching for a roommate and then a cheaper place to live, Marcos conceded the inevitable: Luki would have to move back with her parents until he could find a better job. Until then, Marcos himself would lodge in the monkey house, recently vacated when the zoo sold its troop to a circus in order to raise funds to make repairs on the very same monkey house.

Luki waited four months without hearing news of Marcos— she even wrote him twice—until one day she read the front-page story in *La Extra*, the weekly newspaper that her father bought especially for its last page, which featured large-breasted women above religious messages such as "God had big plans when he made Dora." Under a headline proclaiming "Monkey Man" was a picture of Marcos, swinging on a tire in the monkey house. The story said that after sleeping for several months in the cage, Marcos had begun to act like a monkey. There was, at first, some controversy about allowing him to continue, but the exhibit was enormously popular, and as the zoo director noted, he was eating better than he ever had. Visitors, however, were discouraged from heeding the monkey man's demand to "throw beer."

After seeing the story, Luki's father said, "Never did like monkeys." Then, touching her swelling stomach, he said, "I hope it's an orangutan."

Luki's son, born soon after her father died, was small and had tiny patches on his skin, which the doctor told her was the result of a potassium deficiency. This, the doctor said, could be cured by feeding him bananas. Luki, however, refused to feed her son bananas, and his patches grew until he was old enough to crawl, at which point he made secret pilgrimages to the market. There, he begged bananas from Doña Leti, who called him "my little gorilla."

After their mother left, Karla and her sisters used to stand in the park at quarter after six in the evening and wait for her bus. They waited every evening for a week until the two younger girls decided their mother wasn't coming back, at least not without telling them first. But Karla maintained her vigil for several months.

Even a year later, Karla became excited when she heard the groaning sound of the bus entering town from the highway. If Karla was anywhere near the park she would run to where she could see the bus—a faded white orchid painted on the front— deposit its few passengers on the streets of Santa Cruz amid a black cloud of exhaust. Several times she thought she saw her mother step off, but when she walked, hurriedly and hopefully, to get a clearer view, she was disappointed. It was only Doña Luvia or Doña Silvia, home from visiting relatives in the capital.

Karla's mother was farther away than just the capital. She was living and working in a town called Chicago in the United States of America. Karla knew that to return, her mother would have to travel longer than just the four hours it took for the bus to go from the capital to Santa Cruz. She would ride on an airplane, and although airplanes were said to be very fast, Karla figured it would take at least two days for a plane to fly from Chicago to the capital. Maybe three. Chicago was very far away. But once she was in the capital, she would have to take the bus. And there was just one bus that came into Santa Cruz from the capital. One day, Karla knew, her mother would be on the bus.

When his wife left to live in the United States, Armando was terrified. To his brother Federico, who noticed his feelings, he said he was simply worried about his wife and whether she would make it safely across the Mexican border. It was a dangerous trip, entering illegally into the United States, and he and his wife had both acknowledged the possibility that something terrible could happen to her. In reality, concern for his wife's well-being was only part of Armando's terror. At the heart of it was the thought that, after eleven years of marriage, he was alone.

When, two months after his wife's departure, Armando received a letter from her saying that she had entered the United States safely and was living with a family from Cobán, his terror did not subside, and his brother noticed this.

"Why are you white like a gringo?" Federico asked.

"Maribel doesn't have a job yet," Armando said to explain his fear.

Four months later he received a letter from Maribel saying that she had found work as a maid in the home of a rich family and was living with them and caring for their three-year-old twins. But as Armando was drinking coffee in his brother's house, he tilted the cup against his chin and poured coffee into his lap.

"That's the third time this week," Federico said. "What's wrong with you?"

"My wife has work, but I'm worried they won't pay her," he said. "She's illegal, you know, and they can threaten to deport her. Pay her nothing and threaten to deport her. I've heard stories."

At the end of the year, Armando received his wife's first check, worth three hundred U.S. dollars; this was twice as much as Armando made in a month at his job at the electrical dam. To celebrate, Armando and his brother bought a pint of rum and sat in Federico's living room with the lights low and the radio on. When Armando took a glass from his brother, he dropped it. The sound of its shattering woke Federico's wife, a strict Evangelical. Smelling the alcohol, she ordered her husband and her brother-in-law into the night.

It was raining as Armando and Federico stood under the over-hang of Federico's tin roof.

"This is your fault," Federico said.

"No, this is my wife's fault," Armando said. "If she were here, I'd be sitting in my living room now, listening to my radio and drinking my rum."

He began to cry and stepped into the rain so that his brother could not see his face.

Federico grabbed his brother by the shoulder and said, "What's wrong, Armando?"

"I don't have a wife, Lico," he said. "And my children don't have a mother. We sit around the table in silence. It's like she died."

Over the succeeding months, however, Armando's terror grad-ually gave way to a new feeling of wonder. What he had been frightened of, his aloneness, was not, after all, so horrible. He grew to like the nights when his children would fall asleep and he would sit with his glass of rum in the living room and listen to the radio. He would sometimes sit like that for hours, stroking his newly grown mustache, and no one could tell him it was time to go to bed. And no one could hinder him from thinking about Luki, the woman down the street.

Luki had not expected the silence. When she walked into the market, even the chickens grew quiet, as if they, too, had been discussing her story. She walked around town with a certain swift dignity, buying what she needed in noiseless stores, then retreated to her house. Her house, too, was quiet after her father's death. Her mother spent most of her days huddled in bed, occasionally moaning about how cold she felt, and Luki, bored and in need of money, began making strawberry *helados* to sell to the children who, curious, always gathered outside her door.

At times, she missed her husband, and on certain nights, cold in her bed, she even envisioned herself joining him in the monkey cage, although she could not imagine that the floor of the cage was comfortable. Besides, the thought of exposing her son to such a life was abhorrent. She wanted her son to be a success, not a failed fool like her husband. And on top of it, her husband didn't even recollect his former life. *La Extra* reported that he had lost his ability to communicate in Spanish but was now making sounds that zoological experts said were exactly like those made by monkeys from the *alouatta* species. The zoo's director was even considering introducing a female howler into his cage, partly, *La Extra* said, to spice up the exhibit, which people had grown bored with.

Luki wondered if she herself were losing her ability to speak. Her efforts to communicate with her son in a normal fashion had failed; he seemed to understand only when she spoke to him with "oow-ah-ahs." Besides her son, there was no one, really, to talk to.

One morning, shopping in the dead silent market, she turned quickly after buying sweet potatoes, which she had read were rich in potassium, and collided with Armando Sierra, who dropped the six apples he was holding.

"I'm sorry," he said.

"No, I'm sorry," she said. "I'm still holding my sweet potatoes and I've made your apples fall all over the floor."

She helped him gather up his apples. He thanked her and, in a further gesture of appreciation, went to touch her shoulder, but as he did so, his apples again fell to the floor. More apologies followed; then Luki and Armando laughed.

After Karla's mother left, Karla's father hired a woman from the village of Acamal to cook for the family, and Karla knew her father was not happy with the way the woman cooked. She put too much salt in the eggs; and after he complained, too little salt in the eggs. And, criminally, she sometimes burned the tortillas and at other times served them too cold. She was, however, the only woman he could find at the price he could pay.

When her mother was home, Karla had helped her in the kitchen, slicing vegetables. She even had started learning how to *tortillar*, although she had not had a promising start. The *masa* felt as thick as mud in her hands, and she could not slap it into thin patties like her mother's but laid it on the *comal* in thick, hamburger-sized chunks, which produced oversized tortillas burned on the outside and undercooked within. Even Oso, the dog, refused Karla's tortillas.

Her mother had once grown so frustrated with Karla's cooking that she slapped Karla, and Karla didn't come into the kitchen for three days. When she returned, however, her mother showed her again how to scoop up just a little of the *masa* in her hand and smash it in her palms to get the right, thin plate of tortilla to lay on the hot *comal*. Karla made two good tortillas that night, and they sat in the plastic basket on the table with her mother's tortillas. Her father ate her tortillas with the same indifference he did Karla's mother's, and this made Karla happier than she'd ever been.

But her mother left, and the woman who cooked for the family had her own daughter, who helped peel vegetables and made tortillas without any effort at all, although she couldn't have been more than eight years old. The girls learned young when they lived in the villages, Karla thought, especially the *indígena* girls. They needed to learn because they would marry young, at fourteen or fifteen years old. Cooking was part of the *indígena* marriage ritual. The potential bride had to make a meal for the groom's parents, and if the meal was acceptable, she was welcomed into the family. This seemed to Karla a lot to ask of a fourteen-year-old girl, but that was village *costumbre*.

Karla's father didn't want her to get married, at least not when she was fourteen. He expected her to complete high school, and if she showed enough promise, perhaps even college. But she didn't need to worry about this yet; she had just started her first year in the junior high school in Santa Cruz.

Despite her father's hopes, she wasn't a good student. It was hard to focus on the classes, which started just after lunch and ended at five after six. By the time of her third class, English, she was concentrating on the slice of blue sky between the heavyset gray clouds in the big, wood-frame window above the teacher's desk.

Her English teacher, a man from Cobán, had been to the United States for a year on a scholarship, and one day someone asked him if it was the same time in the United States as in Santa Cruz. The English teacher responded that, yes, the time was the very same, at least in some parts of the United States. The United States was a big country and had what the teacher called "four time zones," and one of its time zones was the same as Santa Cruz's. "So when it's eight o'clock here," the teacher said, "it's eight o'clock in, for instance, Chicago."

Karla looked at her watch. She didn't want to cry, but she did.

After their encounter in the market, Armando and Luki greeted each other whenever they met, greetings which turned sometimes into extended conversations about the weather. Luki, Armando thought, looked a little like his wife. Her skin was light brown with a smattering of freckles, not dark and clear like Maribel's, but she had the same hair: short, thick, and glowing from whatever light was around.

After more than six months of such encounters, Armando finally mustered enough courage to visit Luki, who lived with her mother and young son in a house near a field where everyone from town dumped their trash. Despite its location, Luki's house was clean, with tile floors and white walls.

Luki invited Armando into the large living room, where six chairs arranged in pairs led from a portrait of her father on the wall. Luki pointed to a chair in the second row, behind her chair. Armando sat down and talked to the back of Luki's head because Luki was concentrating on filling plastic bags with strawberry-flavored liquid, which she then put in a freezer and sold for twenty-five centavos. Armando was enveloped in strawberry, a smell that clung to everything, including, pleasantly enough, his skin.

After hearing Armando's story, Luki knew it was not Armando's fault that his wife had left. Some women are born birds, and Armando had been stupid or brave enough to let his go. Luki could feel his breath on her neck, and it was warm, and she knew she could feel his breath every day without thinking anything but how warm it felt.

After hearing Luki's story, Armando knew that her predicament was not her own doing but God's inscrutable will. Sometimes God treats people like circus performers, he thought. And it probably makes for a good show, but only God enjoys it.

Karla was now doing the cooking in her father's house. Their cook quit when her brother fell ill with cholera and the cook had to take care of him. The brother recovered, but the cook had cholera and the brother was taking care of her. Karla was glad the cook was gone, although she wasn't happy that cholera had come to Santa Cruz, come with such severity that the principal of the junior high school was organizing an anticholera parade. Karla was supposed to play a doctor in a skit, and she felt silly wearing a cardboard stethoscope. She was a woman now, the female head of her household. She didn't have to pretend she was a doctor, even if she did like how she looked after putting on the white gown. She had a real job. She learned to make her father's favorite meals, learned from remembering what her mother had made and how she had made it. Sometimes she squinted, as if she were actually staring into the past, and saw her mother at the stove, the wood burning below the *comal*. Or she would ask Doña Luvia or Doña Silvia, ask them as one woman would to another, with all the seriousness of her new responsibilities: "How much oil do I put in when I make fried chicken?" And they would answer her without the least condescension.

She learned. She ruined the fried chicken twice before she got it right, but once she got it right—the skin a little greasy, the way her father liked it—she never got it wrong. And she made him eggs and beans the way he liked, the eggs a little runny and the beans mashed like potatoes. Her greatest pleasure was when her father held up his empty plate and asked, "Any more left?" Tamales with *chipilín*. Chow mien with fried carrots, tomatoes, and peppers. She learned. "Any more left?"

It had been several months since Armando had first set foot in Luki's house and he had gotten tired of talking to the back of her head, despite the pleasant nature of their conversations. He decided that in order to sit next to her without implying anything intimate, he would volunteer to help her fill the plastic bags with strawberry liquid. She accepted, and the two of them sat in the front row of her parlor, scooping out the liquid, although Armando had to use a spoon because Luki had just one ladle.

With a spoon, it took him twice as long to fill a bag, but he didn't mind. He was close to her, her strawberry smell surrounding him like a garden. He marveled at how she could talk and work at the same time, a skill at which he was not adept. Twice, as he was responding to a question, he spilled strawberry liquid on his pants. The third time he did this, he said, "I'm sorry, I'm wasting your liquid." Luki turned to him, noticed the strawberry spots on his pants and smiled. She had all white teeth except one that had a gold star on it, a fancy filling. Light struck the gold star and it shone as brilliant as any star in the sky. She said, "That's all right," and dumped a ladleful of strawberry liquid on her lap. "There," she said, "we're the same." He laughed and they continued to fill the bags.

He spilled some liquid again, and she noticed and dumped more liquid on herself. Later he again spilled liquid on himself. She turned to him and smiled, her brilliant star smile, and lifted the pot of liquid over her head and began to pour it on her hair. The liquid rolled down her forehead and nose. He said, "Stop, you're making a mess of yourself," and tried to wipe the liquid off her face with his fingers. He felt his fingers tingle, deliciously, and he realized she was licking them, kissing them. She kissed the palm of his hands and his wrist as the last of the liquid fell over her.

He withdrew his hand. The strawberry liquid had already dried in spots on her face. Damp strings of hair hung across her lips. He removed them, pushing them back over her forehead, but they fell in the same place. He did this again, and again they fell, and she laughed. He left them, admired them before he bent and, through the damp strings of her hair, kissed her. She responded passionately, pushing the strings of her hair into his mouth with her tongue.

Seconds later he eased her, with all the romance he had forgotten in his wife's absence, into the puddle of strawberry liquid on the floor.

One afternoon, Karla's father told her, "You don't have to cook tonight, Luki's coming over to do it." He smiled as though he had given her a present. Karla went to her room and cried.

She knew about her father and Luki. For more than two years, he had been going over to her house. She heard what everyone said about them, that they were *novios*, even though they both were married.

Karla saw Luki in the streets and market, and Luki always made a point of saying hello to her, but Karla didn't like Luki. Luki was ugly. She had disgusting freckles. And her son was a chimpanzee. She didn't know why her father liked Luki, and she didn't ask him. It wasn't her place to ask. It didn't matter. Her father didn't stay very long at Luki's house anyway. He always came home for dinner. And if he went out again, it was usually to uncle Federico's. But if it wasn't, if he went back to visit Luki, he still was home before Karla and her sisters went to bed. Sometimes he'd sit on the edge of Karla's bed, and he smelled a little funny, like strawberries, but it was a sweet smell, and she tasted strawberries as she fell asleep.

Luki came over with her son, the boy who always smelled like bananas and had hair growing out of his ears, and went into the kitchen and blew the coals until they sparked and added the wood one log at a time until she had the flames burning high and hot. Karla stood next to her, not saying a word, even when Luki asked her something. She thought that she must seem like her mother's ghost, tall and proud. She was her mother's ghost, she decided. She would haunt this woman. The kitchen was her mother's. And if not her mother's, then hers. The last of Luki's questions— "You're going to study one day at the university, aren't you?"— fell unanswered into the fire.

Luki began to smack the *masa*, and Karla wanted to laugh at how clumsily she did it, how methodically, not the way Karla knew, not the speedy thwack, thwack, thwack, her hands turning the lump of corn into a thin circle in seconds. Luki batted the corn with a delicacy Karla found repulsive. The blob of corn eventually became a tortilla, but the method, Karla knew, was all wrong; her mother would have disapproved, too.

Luki's dress, Karla noticed, was made of thin synthetic material and it flapped in the draft that, despite Karla's father's efforts to seal the house, entered the kitchen.

A log with one end aflame fell to the floor and Karla picked it up. She did not return it to the fire. After warning Karla to be careful, Luki turned back to her cooking. Karla lifted the log like a torch, then lowered it under Luki's dress. Horrified and delighted, Karla watched as the dress caught fire and Luki raced, screaming, out of the house, her son bounding after her.

———

Armando's wife had long ago stopped sending him money, but for three successive years before Easter she sent him a letter saying that she was coming home, and in every letter, she gave the name of the airline company, the flight number, and the date and time of arrival. She would conclude her letter the same way, "It has been a long time, and finally I will see my beloved husband and daughters." After receiving the letter, Armando would inform Karla and her sisters and take the first bus from Cobán, swaying with it around the curves, feeling ill, he didn't know whether from nervousness or nausea. He would get to the airport an hour early and have a soda at the overpriced refreshment stand, then stake out a place on the floor above the baggage area, where everyone waited for incoming passengers.

The pilots and flight attendants would pass, with their brisk walk and compact suitcases. Then the passengers would come, old men in shorts and women in ugly hats they had bought in Miami. Inevitably he would see a woman with shoulder-length hair, combed smooth enough for the dim lights to shine off it brilliantly, and his heart would fire against his chest like the recoil of a gun, and he would think: "She's come. She's come." The woman would turn, and he would see that the face was not Maribel's; it was too light a face, and the lips not large enough. He would wait until the last passenger, usually some tall businessman who had probably been delayed inside changing money, came out, took his bags, which a porter would have already removed from the conveyer belt, and marched toward the customs area. Armando would walk to the airlines booth upstairs and ask if his wife had been on the plane, and they would give him the same answer: "We can't say."

Armando didn't miss his wife in the way he had at first, when he could feel her absence as an absence within his body, as if an organ quite near his heart had been removed and a cavity had been left that the wind rushed through until he wanted to cry. Over the years, that cavity had been filled, he didn't know whether with Luki and her strawberry liquid or simply with the dust of time. But he clung to a certain images of his wife, like the way the light reflected off her finely combed hair, and the thought that she and he had come together for a reason, that their bond, initiated, though it may have been, because of lust and curiosity, was holy, and that it, like anything holy, could be resurrected.

If he thought about it, which he was reluctant to do, Armando imagined that his wife sent him these letters out of her own sense of guilt for abandoning what was holy. Perhaps she even wanted to come home, at least in part, but circumstances prevented it. If he thought about it hard, Armando suspected that his wife had done what his brother sometimes teasingly suggested: married a gringo. Her letters, he decided, were her way of assuaging her guilt, connecting to the past while still living the life she had chosen.

When for the fourth year in a row he received a letter from his wife before Easter, he decided to go to the airport, but he vowed that this would be the last time.

Karla knew her mother would come this time. Of all the years her mother had been gone, this was the year Karla needed her most. This was the year she was to turn fifteen. This was the year she was to become a woman. And how could she become a woman without her mother there? How could she go to the church service and receive the priest's blessing without her mother beside her? And this was the year that horrible woman, that Luki, and her horrible son, had stepped into their home. Her mother would come and would see her into womanhood and would keep Luki out, although Karla had done a magnificent job of it herself; Luki had not stepped foot in their house since Karla had set her dress on fire.

Karla and her sisters were waiting in the square at a quarter after five. The bus had never come so early, but for such an important occasion Karla thought it might. Karla and her sisters huddled against the cold on a bench under the town hall. Rain had started as a light sprinkle, a mist almost, but as night approached, it became fiercer and the wind blew damp on them. After half an hour, her sisters crossed the street to play in the park. Karla saw them chase each other around, then go home.

The bus was late. To the west, she could see the last sliver of light between the mountain tops and cloud cover, a strip as thin as a smile. It disappeared quickly.

Then she heard it, the sound like her father clearing his throat, but amplified as if over a microphone. She saw the bus appear, like some monstrous fish, its two eyes beaming in the black, wet night. The bus hissed and stopped. The door opened. Her father stepped out.

She looked behind him. The door closed. Where is she? she wanted to ask, but when she looked at her father's face, she didn't. He was crying. No, it was the rain. Of course it was the rain. He wrapped his arms around her. She felt his heart tremble. "It's cold," he said.

———————

Luki felt wounded by what Karla had done to her—although racing home lit up like a comet, she had felt warmer than she had in years—and she was angry for a while. But she didn't blame Karla; she knew what it was like to be left alone. And it was all right if Karla didn't like her yet, she decided, because she and Karla had more in common than their heartache. Luki looked like Karla, or vice versa, and to Luki, this promised great things, although she wondered at the same time if she were being too hopeful.

She didn't want to hurt Karla, yet she didn't want to surrender what she had won—a promise of more than endless afternoons and evenings filling plastic bags with strawberry liquid.

When Armando again asked her to cook at his house, she accepted, but with a nervous heart.

———————

Yes, it would be all right this time, Karla told her father. Yes, Luki could come to dinner. Luki could make dinner. Yes, she would help. No, she wouldn't burn Luki this time. And she would be nice to Luki's little monkey, mm, son.

Her mother was never coming back, her father had said the night he stepped off the bus. Her mother was never coming back, and they would just have to accept it.

But did she have to accept Luki? Karla wouldn't accept Luki, but she wouldn't burn her again.

When Luki came to make dinner, her dress was wet, as if she'd bathed with it on. Armando asked her what had happened—it wasn't raining—and Luki said, "I'm fireproof," and winked.

Even after she had made dinner, laboring in front of the burning wood, she was still damp, and Karla knew Luki felt cold, because every so often she shivered, even after she drank three cups of scalding coffee. Before the last of the beefsteak was eaten, Luki was shaking violently. "You've caught a cold," Armando said, and Luki could not even say yes because her teeth were chattering.

With a graciousness she did not think herself capable of, Karla offered Luki her bed, and Armando brought her one of his wife's old nightgowns, one Karla remembered, with sheep on the shoulders. Luki huddled beneath the rough wool blankets in Karla's bed. Her son had been put in Armando's bed. It was just after eight, but everyone, exhausted, had decided to go to sleep. Karla sat in a chair near the wall.

"Where're you going to sleep?" Luki asked her.

"I'm not going to sleep," Karla said.

"You can sleep here with me."

"I'm not tired."

Karla watched the frequency and intensity of Luki's shivers decrease, and then she heard a faint whistling sound, Luki's sleep breathing, a pleasant sound, vaguely familiar. Karla put her head against the wall. She really was tired. But she'd rather sleep in the rain than sleep with Luki.

She heard Luki turn over in bed, and it jarred her awake. Karla had been sleeping. How long? Her bones ached. And she felt she was catching a cold. She sniffled, then started to cry. It was cold. Maybe she would crawl into bed with her sisters. But they had just a single bed for the two of them. If she got in, one would fall on the floor and bawl. No, Karla thought, better to sleep in the chair.

She stopped crying. Her bones ached still. And she was cold. Uncomfortable. Cold. Cold. She felt herself being lifted, as in a dream. Less cold now. Warm, even. She stretched, and her feet and hands were warm. Better. Sleep. Deep into sleep. Into the deep, deep of sleep, like deep into a warm hole, feeling what rabbits must feel, crawling into their holes.

When Karla woke up, the sun was in her eyes, and Luki's arms were around her. They were in Karla's bed. Luki was crying. "Why are you crying?" Karla asked.

"It's warm," Luki said.

"Yes," Karla agreed. "It's warm."

The
Corner
Kick

The goalie tipped the ball over the crossbeam, then fell into the net. He wiggled, wrapping himself tighter. He clutched his knee.

A doctor in a bright pink jacket jogged onto the field. "*Denlo espacio,*" the doctor said to the players crowding around the goalie. The players crowded closer. Muttering, the doctor opened his case and pulled out a pair of scissors. He cut the net. Free, the goalie continued to wiggle in pain.

Juan jogged to the left corner of the field, where the ball awaited him. There were four minutes left in the game. With his hands, he set up the ball the way he always did, on a tuft of grass. He liked the advantage this gave him; he could sweep under the ball and lift it almost straight up.

A high kick favored his team because of its forwards. They were as tall as basketball players and could jump, too. He'd often watched his high passes meet one of their foreheads and, in what seemed like the same moment, settle into the back of the net. Sometimes Juan knew when this would happen because of the way the ball came off his foot. If it felt light and pliant and if it whistled slightly in the air, he knew. On these occasions, Juan watched the inevitable unfold with furious beauty.

"Who's winning?" someone asked behind him.

He turned around. Above him was a boy, probably nine years old, manning the scoreboard.

"Did you ask who's winning?"

"Yes," the boy said.

"You're keeping score. You should know we're down a goal."

"Yes, I guess I did know."

Juan figured the boy must have wanted to talk, and his question was the only one he could think of to initiate conversation. Juan smiled, knowing the boy probably adored him with the same devotion he would one day admire a girl.

"Do they pay you to keep score?" Juan asked.

"Sometimes."

"Why not all the time?"

"Sometimes they forget. And sometimes I forget to ask them. My mother gets angry with me."

"Is your mother here today?"

"No, she's at home. We live in Santa Cruz."

Santa Cruz was the last town they had passed through before arriving at the field in San Cristóbal. Santa Cruz was also the town where Juan had grown up. When the team's bus passed through Santa Cruz, Juan had slouched in his seat so only his hair was visible in the window. Juan's mother lived in Santa Cruz, but he hadn't spoken to her in ten years.

Juan looked to see if the goalie had risen. The doctor in the pink jacket was bent over him, spreading cream on the goalie's knee. The other players, once so interested in the goalie's trauma, had drifted to other parts of the field. *Vámanos*, Juan thought.

Juan didn't want to think about his corner kick. If he thought about it, he wouldn't do well. Better to think about women.

"How old's your mother?" Juan asked the boy.

"I don't know."

"How about your father?"

"I don't have a father."

"What happened to him?"

"He left."

A thought occurred to Juan: I'm the boy's father.

Ten years before, he had left his pregnant girlfriend, Blanca, in Santa Cruz. His mother and her father insisted he marry her. This was the proper thing. To marry her, though, would have meant quitting soccer—at eighteen, he was one of the town's best players—and getting a job. He didn't marry her. Instead he moved away to play soccer.

He'd heard Blanca had left town not long after he did. In a new place she could concoct a story. Yes, my husband died. And I am left alone with our child. A *viuda* attracts universal sympathy, a *madre soltera* merely the wanton attention of hungry men.

Juan didn't know if the baby she had was a boy or girl, or even if she'd had the baby. When he thought about it, which was rare, he liked to think Blanca had miscarried.

A week after Blanca told him she was pregnant, he received a telegram from the coach of Palencia, asking him to sign on. Palencia, a town two hundred kilometers from Santa Cruz, had a team in League C, the lowest professional league. The team offered Juan enough money to live on. He showed the telegram to his mother and she tore it up, saying, "You must do what's right." His mother had converted to Evangelism after his father left, and her love had turned hard. She was willing to forgive him, but only if he married Blanca. He left without saying good-bye.

He played in Palencia for two seasons before Escuintla, a team in League B, signed him. He played in Escuintla for six years, earning good money and frequent photos in *El Gráfico*. He scored a goal in the League B championship game, but his team lost, missing its opportunity to advance to League A. The next year, he wasn't on the starting team, and when the season ended he was not re-signed.

He asked around, but no team in League B wanted him. He

called the owner of Palencia and returned to his old team and his old salary. He was twenty-eight years old.

The opposing goalie was still down, the doctor still bent over him, examining his eyes.

Juan looked at the ball in front of him, its black pentagons reflecting the sun's bright light. He had always loved the look of a soccer ball, its stark dignity. He could picture it after his kick, leaping into the sky. But he didn't want to think about the corner kick. He turned back to the boy.

"Have you always lived in Santa Cruz?"

The boy shook his head. "I was born in the capital and then we moved to Puerto Barrios."

"Does your mother work?"

"She used to work in the Coca-Cola factory in the capital. Then they sent her to work in the factory in Puerto Barrios. But the water was dirty and the factory got in trouble and so they closed it. Right now we're living with my *abuelita*."

"And you work here to help your mother?"

The boy nodded. "I also shine shoes in the park. Do you want a shoe shine?"

Juan looked at his cleats and laughed. And if this is my son? he thought. A funny boy. It would be nice to have a funny boy as a son.

He'd loved Blanca, but in a silly, hedonistic way, the way he loved a cool bath in the river or a beer. She had thick black hair that curled away from her round, dark face and a nose he found attractive despite how long it was. He celebrated her without any special appreciation. She was part of the flow of his youth, which offered him so many pleasures.

Her mother and father were divorced, a rare phenomenon in town. Even rarer, she lived with her father, who spent half the week working in the capital. She had two younger sisters and was assigned to care for them in her father's absence. On the nights her father was in the capital, she sent her sisters to bed and waited for Juan. He came before midnight and stayed until five in the morning. They sat on a couch in her living room with the lights off, their conversation broken by kisses and his occasional pleas for more, which she refused. He left when he heard the day's first bus roar through town. He had to return home before his mother woke.

One night, sitting on the couch, they heard her father's car. He'd gone to the capital that morning and Blanca hadn't expected him back for two days. The sound of his motor, though, was unmistakable: it coughed like a dog having trouble with a bone.

Juan couldn't risk leaving through the front door, and there was no other way out of the house. Blanca pushed him out of her living room and ran to her bedroom. The house was dark, and Juan stumbled down the hallway and into the courtyard, enclosed by high walls with broken glass cemented to the top, to prevent thieves from entering. The moonlit courtyard was not a good place to be. Juan crouched under the *pila*, its faucet dripping into the basin of water.

Juan heard two voices, Blanca's father's, then a woman's, hers more melodic, like a song played on low volume. They didn't come into the courtyard but went quietly to his room. Juan heard someone open the window above the *pila*, pushing aside its solid wood covering. He heard them discussing the long drive from the capital. Then their voices were replaced by more passionate sounds, the meshing of lips, and he heard Blanca's father groan and plead faintly. He heard the woman breathing heavily, as if running, and then Blanca's father groan again. He heard a faint panting, hardly audible above the steady drip of water. Then he heard Blanca's father snore, the loudest sound of the night.

Juan sighed. He was about to leave his hiding place when he heard a patter of feet. From beneath the *pila*, he could see the woman only from her waist down. She wore nothing, and he marveled at the silky triangle of her pubic hair, the moonlight illuminating its dampness.

She approached the *pila*. Juan's nose was within an inch of her thighs, and although he tried to hold his breath, he could smell her. She smelled like ripe bananas, only tarter.

The woman washed, splashing cold water from the *pila's* basin on her thighs and knees and feet. She brought a towel between her legs and cleaned herself. Then she was gone, and in a minute, he heard the window close above him.

On his next visit to Blanca's house, Juan didn't stop kissing Blanca when she spoke to him. She seemed at first delighted by his forceful kisses. He covered her neck with them. But when he removed her bra, she said, "No, Juan." He didn't stop, though, and he pulled off her T-shirt. More gently, he kissed her breasts, pleased with how large they were. When he looked up at her, she was looking away. He told her he loved her, and that this is what people who loved each other did. She didn't protest, although she said nothing and didn't move when he lowered her on the couch and removed her skirt and underwear and pushed himself into her. His pleasure lasted seconds.

He returned the next night, feeling guilty, and tried to talk to her as he had before, with the same joking spirit, but he knew things would never be the same. She mentioned marriage, and he mumbled agreement, and they made love. This time she didn't cry.

By the time she told him she was pregnant, his visits to her house had all but stopped. He was interested in another girl.

The doctor in the pink jacket waved to the sidelines, and two men raced onto the field, carrying a stretcher. They set the stretcher beside the goalie, and went to lift him onto it—one man taking the goalie's shoulders, the other his ankles—but the goalie said something and the doctor said something and the men let go of the goalie and stood behind the doctor.

Juan looked at the boy, who wasn't gazing at the field any more, but at the lake down the hill. The boy, Juan decided, looked like Blanca. He had her wavy hair and long nose, and his eyes were the same—small and dreamy. But the boy had a square build, like Juan, and long legs. Yes, Juan decided, the boy would grow as tall as he, and perhaps as handsome. Women would love him.

Like most soccer players, even mediocre ones, Juan had had many women. He visited whorehouses with his fellow players and learned to like the routine. First, they sat in a central room, drinking beers and conversing about a practice or game. Then the women were released, as if from a corral. They came from a single large door to sit on the players' laps and kiss their cheeks and encourage them toward the private rooms. One night, to show off, Juan made love to a woman right at the table as his teammates watched, sat her on his waist, screwed and drank at the same time. When he'd finished, he followed another woman to a room.

His story spread to locker rooms across the country, but his days of whoring ended that night. The next afternoon, when he went to piss, he felt fire. Even after the team doctor shot him full of penicillin, he wasn't cured, and he didn't drink much, dreading the pain. During the team's visit to Morales, he had to miss the game; instead of playing he lay in a hot clinic, with an IV dripping into him. The doctor administered him more drugs, but he couldn't beat his gonorrhea. On the way back to Escuintla, the team dropped him and a teammate off in Zacapa. His teammate, a *Zacapateco*, took Juan to his grandmother, who lived in a crumbling adobe house between *tiendas* painted with Pepsi emblems. The grandmother concocted something out of eggs, coconuts, and what she called *jugo de culebra*. It tasted like sour milk, and Juan had trouble downing the entire glass. The fire in his groin, however, soon disappeared.

Scared of disease, he became a faithful lover in the only way a *mujeriego* can, remaining with the same woman for a certain time—longer, that is, than a night. He consumed women with less urgency than before, deciding that a thorough exploration of their bodies could not be achieved in a night. Additionally, these women offered him something he had grown to covet as much as sex: words.

They flattered him with their giggles and winks and laughter, but mostly they flattered him with lavish, loving words, extolling his soccer talents and, by extension, he thought, his person, his soul.

The two men picked up their stretcher and shuffled off the field. The doctor in the pink jacket pointed to certain places on the goalie's leg and the goalie either nodded or shook his head.

Juan turned again to the boy. "Do you go with your friends to the lake?"

Still staring at the lake, which looked almost ice covered because of the bright afternoon light, the boy shook his head.

"When I lived here, my friends and I used to take rowboats onto the lake," Juan said. "We'd rent them from an old man who lived over there." The boy glanced at him, and Juan pointed to pine trees on the south side of the lake. "I'm sure he still lives there. Probably has the same boats."

Juan thought it would be nice to take the boy, his son, on a rowboat on the lake. They could explore the reeds on the west side, see what kinds of ducks they could scare.

"I don't know how to swim," the boy said.

Juan was about to tell the boy it didn't matter—the rowboat was safe, the water gentle—but he didn't.

In Palencia, Juan lived in a hotel, paid for by the team, and the hotel had a swimming pool, a meter-deep circle in the patio. The pool was the first thing he showed new women, strolling them around it as if he were introducing them to some precious artifact. The pool looked more inviting than it actually was. Even on days it did not reek of chlorine, the pool was lukewarm. Nevertheless, it was the most impressive aspect of his life, more impressive than his dwindling soccer skills.

His latest *novia*, Lilian, was a small woman with a mole above her lip and hair that, when they made love, covered her breasts. He'd been with her for five months, unprecedented for him. Two weeks before the game in San Cristóbal, though, she had not visited him when she was supposed to, and he surprised himself by pacing around his room like someone waiting in a hospital. He watched the clock on his wall and cursed every languid minute that passed. At nine o'clock, he decided to find another woman, even if it meant returning to a whorehouse, and he opened his door and stepped into the night. As often happened, there were no guests in the hotel, and the lights around the pool were turned off. He stepped to the edge of the pool, hoping to see the stars reflected in it. There were no clouds in the sky but few stars either, and none were reflected in the pool, which seemed gray and murky. Playing with his fear, he moved so his shoe tips hung over the pool. Then he lost his balance. It didn't matter that he couldn't swim; he could stand without problem. But in that instant of falling, he felt hopeless, and struggling to find the bottom of the pool with his feet, he knew how easy it would be to die.

Lilian came the next day, full of apologies: her mother was sick, her brother had been in a motorcycle accident. He didn't believe her, wanted to challenge her, call her a liar. But he was grateful that she was with him again, that he could touch her, mostly that she would speak to him in the phrases that he liked and needed to believe.

It was before he was to leave for the San Cristóbal game, the last game of the season, that he told her he loved her. He'd said this to many of the women he'd been with, even to some prostitutes, but when he said these words to Lilian, they conveyed more than he'd meant them to. They were, he knew, full of his need, his fear, his longing. He wouldn't be playing soccer much longer—he worried he wouldn't be re-signed even the next season—and he knew he would need her to keep speaking to him of how great he was and would be. He resented how much he needed her. That night he tried to hurt her; with both of them naked, he threw her on her stomach and climbed on top of her. But he wasn't hard, and with his limp cock nestled between the crack of her buttocks, he lay on her back and cried.

She rolled over to face the wall and he curled next to her and clung to her as a monkey does to the last branch above a long fall.

The goalie stood up, hopped a little to test his knee, nodded. Smiling, the doctor in the pink jacket trotted off the field. The referee signaled for Juan to kick. Juan didn't move. He was looking at the boy, who had turned back to the field. If he was the boy's father—and he must be—then he would return to the boy's mother. He would grab hold of his new responsibility. His soccer days were done, but he had a new plan, a new arena in which to shine. He would return, a wiser man, to be with Blanca, to love the boy they had created long ago. He would raise the boy, teach him to play soccer, send him to school, and he would care for Blanca because of the hardship he had caused her. She would forgive him and love him more than she would have had he married her ten years before.

The crowd chanted. The referee gave Juan a stern look. He turned to the boy. "What's your mother's name?" Juan asked.

The boy smiled. "Juana."

Juan had already planned what he was going to do: leave his spot in the corner, call to the coach to send in a replacement. He was going to talk to the boy, to tell him he was his father, to begin this new phase of his heroism. But the boy had said Juana—only a letter different from his own name—and Juan felt betrayed. He wondered if this weren't a scheme or joke, the goalie's injury a facade, an act to give him time to talk with the boy and revisit his past, to unnerve him.

His teammates were yelling at him. He turned toward the ball propped in the grass. He took two swift steps and kicked. The ball felt light against his foot, but too light, and it flew too high and long, sailing over his teammates and clear to the other side of the field, where it bounced out of bounds.

The goalie clapped, grinning with long teeth, and Juan glared at him, furious at his masquerade, his false display of pain. He wanted to yell at him—*mentiroso, hijo de puta, joto*—but the words didn't come. Instead, Juan felt his throat catch and his eyes fill. He turned toward the boy, seeking another target for his anger—or an invitation in the boy's face, a hopeful expression into which he could project other possibilities: perhaps Blanca had changed her name; maybe the boy, although not his, still needed a father. The boy, though, had turned away from the game and was again staring at the lake.

For a second Juan didn't know what to do. He thought of calling to the boy, asking him something, anything to start a new conversation. But he saw the ball fly toward midfield, and he felt his feet move under him, carving a familiar path up the sideline.

The
Priest's
Daughter

───────────────

       They called her the priest's daughter, but her name was Esther. She lived with her mother in a two-room house on the highway, a fifteen-minute walk from the nearest town, Santa Cruz. The house was made of wood, and when it rained, which it did frequently, the wood bled water. Esther noticed that people were afraid of the rain, to one degree or another. When it rained, the farmers in the nearby fields left their corn and huddled under trees; the women waiting for the bus gathered close and their daughters slipped under their skirts; and the bike riders on the highway parked under the tin roof of Doña Maria's *tienda* and ate jalapeño chips.

       Esther wasn't afraid of the rain. When it rained, she stopped whatever she was doing and stepped into it. One morning Esther left two tortillas cooking on the *comal* and raced into the rain. By the time the rain stopped, the tortillas were blacker than the richest soil. Her mother scolded her but then could not help herself and laughed. "You're crazy," her mother said.

Esther liked how the rain felt when it was light and warm and caressed the roots of her long black hair. She didn't like it as much when clouds rumbled into each other like heavy trucks and released a rain that came with relentless fury. But she joined this rain, too, staying in it until it ended. She felt she had a purpose in the rain, although she did not know what it was.

She was a priest's daughter, and she had known this ever since she had understood words. Her mother had been a cook at the parish in Santa Cruz. By the time Esther was born, however, the priest was gone, off to repent at the feet of some higher priest, and her mother had to look for other work. Her mother became a maid at a house in Cobán, the city north of Santa Cruz, and when the woman in the house grew jealous of her and dismissed her, she worked picking coffee and then sorting asparagus.

When she was young, Esther thought her mother might be angry or sad or lonely. But when she was older, Esther knew that because people always called her mother "*pobrecita amante del padre*," she had mimicked their pity. Her mother was not angry or sad or lonely. Her mother walked barefoot on the dirt floor of their house as if it were warm sand on a gold beach, and she celebrated the rain with Esther by smiling and clapping.

Esther and her mother were poor, undeniably, but there were only two of them. Other families with larger incomes lived harder lives because they had more children to feed and send to school. Nevertheless, in elementary school Esther was treated like an outcast by most of her classmates, many of whom wore more ragged clothes than hers. Their scorn, however, did not bother her as it did others who suffered the same treatment. Their teasing seemed to her like so many weeds trying futilely to destroy a tall, strong corn plant.

Esther was friends with other girls who, for reasons of birth or ill-fortune, were shunned. There was Josefina Chinchilla, whose father killed a man in a machete fight in a whorehouse and walked home naked with the man's right arm slung over his shoulder.

Josefina was known, of course, as the "murderer's daughter." There was Alicia De Leon, who had been born with her nose embedded below the surface of her face and whom everyone called No Nose. There was Sandra Gonzales, who as a baby was thrown from the back of a pickup truck and fell into a three-month coma. She grew to be barely four feet tall and her speech was slurred almost beyond comprehension. Her classmates nicknamed her Dwarf Drawl.

Over time, Esther watched them all be destroyed. Josefina Chinchilla had her first boyfriend at age twelve and was no longer a virgin by age thirteen. At fourteen, she got pregnant but miscarried. She miscarried at fifteen and sixteen. When she was seventeen, she led a troop of boys away from Ana Fernandez's fifteenth birthday party and let them have her on the grass above the river. She became pregnant from this encounter, too. When she miscarried again, she rose from her bed and carried the slick, bloody sack around town as possessively as a dog would a bone until a policeman, summoned by an outraged cantina owner, threw her and her dead child in jail. She remained in the outdoor cell all night, sniffing the urine that clung to the walls like paint and watching the puddles from the ferocious rain grow under the bars. She caught a fever and almost died. When she recovered, her mother sent her to live with relatives in a mountain village.

Alicia De Leon, Esther's other friend, suffered cruel jests about how she should join the circus. "Come see the girl with no nose," her tormentors teased. "She smells through her ears, breathes through her eyes, sneezes through her toes." One day, Alicia arrived at school with a mask that covered everything but her eyes and mouth. Her elementary school classmates, on unusually good behavior, said nothing until Erwin Ponce, a stocky boy with a thousand well-groomed curls, drew his own mask on notebook paper, taped it to his face and danced on the top of his desk, shouting, "I'm the mask monster and I need a wife." The laughter made Alicia run from the room as if hunted.

Long after her classmates had repented of their earlier wickedness, when, in fact, many of them had confronted their own tragedies, Alicia did exactly what they had said she should do. When the Frog Brothers, Marcos the Monkey Man, and the other members of the Tall and Tiny Circus came to town, she joined them.

Sandra Gonzales was Esther's best friend, the only one who made it with Esther to high school at Colegio Verapaz on the outskirts of Cobán. Despite her speech problem, Sandra was an excellent student, consistently one of the best in her class. And although she walked with a duck's waddle, she passed physical education, because whereas she failed all the physical exams, like making a layup or dribbling a soccer ball, she wrote book-length reports on the history of volleyball and Ping-Pong, complete with illustrations.

Sandra Gonzales was like Esther in another respect. She liked boys. Worshipped them, feared them, desired them, scorned them, dreamed of them. In her final year of high school, she picked as her object of love the boy every girl had picked. César Juarez was tall and light skinned with a mustache as dark as shoe polish.

Esther loved César Juarez, too, but realized she had no chance to win him. She was a priest's daughter, the tainted product of her mother's seduction of a holy man, and she bore her nickname with serenity. Esther had learned to accept as impossible what most girls considered at least conceivable. She saw potential romance with nobles such as César Juarez in a mystical way. To win his love, she knew, the world would have to behave uncharacteristically, the elements that composed normal life meshing in a strange constellation. But Esther was not unhappy, not at all, and she did not pine even a minute for any unrealized romance. She had had two boyfriends, the most recent of whom was Hector Briones, whose mother had been run over by a tour bus.

Sandra Gonzales did not share Esther's sense of the impossible. She believed not only in the likelihood of miracle but in its certainty. She was sure she would be César Juarez's girlfriend. Esther did nothing to discourage her. Hope, she decided, might be the chief ingredient needed to shake up the elements of normal life, and if Sandra had enough hope, anything might be possible. Esther also liked the role she assumed after her friend's inevitable disappointments. She was ready, with open arms and light words, to comfort, console, and hear her confessions of lucid dreams unfulfilled.

Near the end of the school year, after Sandra Gonzales and Esther had both turned twenty and were about to graduate from Colegio Verapaz, the class took a trip to the lake in San Cristóbal, a town west of Santa Cruz. It was early May, a time when it rained periodically and one could not wake up to a sunny morning with the confidence that it would be sunny at noon. It was, however, sunny when the class arrived on the shores of the lake, carting lunches and soccer balls.

After lunch was eaten and soccer played, a group of boys drifted down the hill to the lake's edge to watch the fish and throw stones in the water. Sandra Gonzales and Esther trailed them like altar boys. They stopped a few feet short and perched on the last grassy hump before the hill became shore, their light dresses flapping in the breeze. The boys' conversation turned to the lake itself and its deceptive distances. While the opposite shore looked close, César Juarez said, it was actually a kilometer away, and the only people known to have swum it were the three men who participated in the first and last San Cristóbal Triathlon, and two of the participants had dropped out after completing the swim. "No one here could do it," he said. "Not even me."

Seconds later, Sandra Gonzales announced what Esther knew was "I can swim it," but the boys must not have understood, or if they did, they must have thought that what she said was not directed at them. Indeed, by the time Sandra made her bold pronouncement, the boys were talking about who had the class's longest index finger. When Sandra kicked off her sandals and rumbled past them, the boys drew back as if a wild animal had burst by. Sandra fell into the lake and began an awkward swim toward the far shore. The boys watched for a minute, then turned their attention to the ranks of clouds coming like an army over the mountains to the south. "Rain," César Juarez said, and even as he said this, the first drop fell. "Rain," another boy said, and the rain came hard now, and the boys abandoned the shore, running up the hill toward the thatched-roofed *comedor* at the top.

The rain pushed Esther's hair in front of her face, and she had to hold it up to see Sandra, who was not even a third of the way across the lake. "Come back!" she yelled at her, but the rain was loud and must have been even louder to Sandra in the water.

Esther thought about water beating water, and the futility of it. She yelled Sandra's name again, but now, because of the ferocity of the rain, she could not see her at all.

The night before Sandra Gonzales's funeral, Esther's mother told Esther about her father, the priest, a story Esther had heard as soon as she could hear. Over the years, her mother had repeated the story, but in different forms, depending on Esther's age. Now Esther was a woman, and her mother spoke to her as a woman.

Her mother used to cook for the priest in the dark kitchen of the rectory. The wood snapped on top of the stove, the big pots rested directly on the fire. The priest often came to sit with her, on a stool just out of the smoke's way, and he would talk about his childhood. As a boy, he was a good soccer player, and he still dreamed of elegant passes and evasive dribbles down the sidelines and the rough admiration of drunk men and the shy devotion of pretty girls. She told him she had always liked soccer, particularly as it was played in the late afternoon. The day cools, but the heat of the game, a heat the players feel, intensifies, and those watching, if they are watching closely, feel the heat as well. "Yes," the priest said. "That's it, exactly." He stood, approached her, but a burst from the fire that sent sparks skipping everywhere stopped him, and he left the kitchen.

Her mother had loved the priest. He was a good priest, and he cared for the words he spoke. He was not like the former priest, whom Esther's mother had also cooked for, who read the Bible as if it were a government report. Her priest spoke each word as a patient child eats chocolate, with nibbles of devotion. He was a good priest, and he cared for the people in the parish. He counseled the sick and troubled in his living room, and at night he left the front room of the rectory open for those who, for whatever reason, could not sleep at home. He visited the villages, and although he was from the capital and had been taught a strict Catholicism by the conservative bishops, he dropped chicken blood around a pile of corn seed and prayed all night with the *indígena* farmers, in their language, for a blessed harvest. She loved the priest, and could not help it if because of her love, she wanted him to love her, and not only in the way he loved God, his words like caresses but still only words.

He was sitting behind the smoke when he told her about how nice it was, as a boy, to take off his shirt and feel the sweat at first creep and then race out of his skin as he ran up and down the field. I know, Esther's mother told him, I used to watch the boys play soccer shirtless after school and their skin would become wet, and when the sunlight hit them right, their bare backs would be brighter than sky. The priest approached her, braving the smoke, and they made love standing in front of the fire.

The priest repented more severely than she could ever have expected. When their lovemaking was over, he placed his hand in the fire and it remained there until she pushed him away.

"People feel sorry for me now," Esther's mother told her, "but for a moment he loved me more than he loved God."

Before Sandra Gonzales's coffin was cemented into the crypt, the rain fell. It fell hard from the first, and the sudden force scared the people at the funeral, even Sandra's mother, and they sprinted for tombs with overhanging roofs.

Esther stayed in the rain with the two men who were smoothing concrete over Sandra's grave. Spreading her fingers to catch the ferocious drops, she felt how sensuous the rain was, even in its quick and furious fall. But Esther knew the sensation of water on her skin alone wasn't why she stood in the rain; it wasn't why Sandra had tried to swim the lake.

The rain flattened Esther's hair, soaked her dress, filled her shoes. The two men finished their work, then raced to join the others. Esther alone remained, drenched, satisfied: she knew everyone was watching her.

Bathwater

I was two days from starting classes at Colegio
Verapaz, thanks to the scholarship I'd won, when my mother
returned from work, drenched from the afternoon rain, and fell
into her bed as if she intended to remain prone on the *petate* forever. I came to her side and began to sing, which I did sometimes
to soothe her aches, but she placed a finger over her mouth and I
fell silent.

"You must work for me, son. I've arranged it with Señor
Prado."

I didn't complain or mention the scholarship or invoke my
dream to become a doctor or a lawyer. I said, "Of course, mother,"
and the next day she brought me with her to María's house.

The work wasn't hard. It was similar to what I did at home—sweep, mainly—except María's house was ten times larger than ours and it had tile floors whereas ours had dirt. I learned how to mop her floors, too, something I'd never done. It wasn't easy; my mother scolded me three times for putting the mop into dirty water. I also learned how to wash and dry María's clothes, although this was simple because of the machines in the kitchen.

The most important thing I had to learn was how to prepare María's bathwater. She took her baths in a big tub on the second floor. Señor Prado had twice installed water heaters, but neither worked and only cold water ran into the bath. María didn't like cold water. My mother didn't mind that María, who was *indígena* like us, wore blue jeans instead of *corte*, or that she wasn't married to Señor Prado and he had a wife. But she found it intolerable that María insisted on bathing in hot water. "Didn't her mother tell her that she'll get sick in hot water?" my mother complained more than once during the week I worked with her. I think my mother, being old, just didn't like to prepare the water on the two six-burner stoves in the kitchen and then carry it up the stairs, pot by pot, to María's bathtub.

We didn't see or even hear María the entire week, yet it was obvious she was present. When we arrived in the morning, used breakfast plates were on the dining room table. And when we went to drain the bathtub, the water smelled sweet.

As we worked, my mother spoke to me about María in whispers, as if María were always in an adjacent room, listening. María, my mother said, was a former *indígena* queen, having won the pageant in Cobán several years before against two hundred contestants from around the country. During the pageant, Señor Prado, who was one of the judges, fell in love with her. A few months later, she became his mistress and he bought her the house outside of Santa Cruz.

Away from the house, however, my mother was reluctant to speak María's name. Walking back to our village at the end of the day, I asked about María—why she was so quiet, why she never appeared—but my mother either pretended not to hear me or ignored my questions by making observations about cornfields we passed or vultures circling a distant carcass.

On my first day of work alone, I felt uncomfortable entering a house whose occupant I'd never met. The house, however, was familiar, and I settled into the routine my mother had taught me.

I began by removing the plate and cup that María had used for breakfast from the table in the dining room, washed them in the kitchen sink, and returned them to a cupboard above the stove. Then I retrieved a broom from the kitchen closet and began sweeping downstairs. I started in the kitchen, where blue pots hung from all four walls. The smallest pots were barely the width of my hand; the largest, when I stood beside them, nearly reached my knees. It was in these large pots that I heated María's bathwater.

I ignored Señor Prado's study, located off the kitchen. Although the study had no door, I was forbidden to enter it. Señor Prado, my mother said, could smell footprints, and he would treat me harshly if I stepped foot in his study. I swept the dining room, where framed clippings from newspapers of brides in long gowns decorated the walls. The women in the photographs were pretty, and I paused to admire them. They were all smiling, although some of their smiles seemed insincere, as if coaxed by the photographer. I swept the hallway, with its varnished wood staircase. I swept the living room, where a stuffed jaguar rested in the corner. The last room contained a collection of rakes, *azadones*, shovels, and a wheelbarrow, all of which, as far as I could tell, had never been used. At the back of the room was a door, opening on the backyard. It was through this door that I entered and exited the house. Out the door I swept the dust I had accumulated from the five rooms downstairs.

I returned to the kitchen and put María's bathwater on to heat. Next I swept upstairs, first in the library, where books filled a tall bookcase, then in the room where María kept her clothes: seven pairs of blue jeans, seven black blouses, seven pairs of black socks, and seven pairs of red underwear. The blue jeans and blouses hung from long hooks on the ceiling. The socks and underwear were kept in crates against a wall.

I cleaned the bathroom next. After sweeping what little dust I had collected with my broom onto the landing, I filled the bucket below the sink with water. I opened the door of the closet beside the sink and removed a mop and soap. I mopped the bathroom twice, as my mother had instructed, to ensure that it was perfectly clean.

There was another room in the house that my mother told me I was forbidden to enter: María's bedroom, next to the bathroom.

I returned downstairs, sweeping the dust from upstairs out the front door. I mopped the kitchen, and when I finished, the bathwater was boiling. I brought the first pot upstairs. I pulled back the blue curtain in front of the bathtub and dumped the water. The bathtub was large—larger than my mother's bed—and deep. I returned downstairs for the second pot. When I had dumped all twelve pots, I turned on cold water. When the bathtub was nearly full, I turned off the water. I stepped onto the landing and announced, "The bathwater's ready." My voice sounded small in the vastness of the house.

I wasn't allowed to stay upstairs while María took her bath. I was supposed to wait in the kitchen for exactly an hour before returning to clean María's bathtub.

It's remarkable what you hear when you're listening intently, as I was. I heard a farmer slap his whip on a horse and a tree branch creak in the wind. I heard a cricket make a lonely daytime plea and a cow complain. I expected to hear splashes of water or María's footsteps as she left the bath. I expected to hear her bedroom door open. I heard nothing from upstairs.

When the hour was over, I carried the mop up the stairs to the bathroom. I swept aside the blue curtain. The bathwater smelled like tangerines. I pulled the plug and watched the water disappear. Then I cleaned the bathtub with mop and soap, running cold water to rinse it. I returned the mop to the closet and picked up the blue jeans, blouse, socks, and underwear that María had left on the floor and walked downstairs to wash them in the machine in the kitchen.

When the clothes had finished washing, I put them in the drying machine. After the buzzer sounded, I took the clothes out of the drying machine and hung them on the line under a tin roof in the backyard. My mother said María liked to smell the air on her clothes. I returned to the room with the *azadones* and shovels and ate the lunch my mother had prepared for me: five tortillas, a bowl of beets, and two hard-boiled eggs with a pepper and tomato sauce.

In the afternoon, I mopped all the rooms downstairs, including the kitchen again, and the library and clothes room upstairs. I finished at four o'clock and returned to the toolroom. My mother said if María wanted anything, she would call me. At five o'clock, I picked María's clothes off the line, huddling over them as I raced out of the rain, and returned them to the clothes room. I hung the blue jeans and blouse from their hooks and folded the socks and underwear and placed them in their crates.

After leaving the clothes room, I stopped beside María's bedroom door to listen. I listened a long time, but I could hear only my blood throbbing against my forehead.

Before beginning work in María's house, I had known girls, of course. When I was young, I listened to them fill the cornfields in the mornings with their giggles. And when I was older and attending El Instituto Básico in Santa Cruz, I used to stare at them from the back of the classroom, admiring the fall of their hair on their backs and the delicate curves of their hands. I was shy, too shy to do what some of my classmates did and actually propose something adventurous to these girls, a trip, say, to Cobán or something dark and pleasurable in the grove of pine trees above the school. I was ignorant of even the simplest facets of their nature, and yet I was curious, enamored, hooked.

I was sixteen when I began work in María's house, and my contact with my school friends (and the girls who enchanted me) was cut off. I worked seven days a week, rising at dawn to make the hour-and-a-half walk down the mountain and returning to my house at dusk. Our village had two dozen families, and if I wasn't exhausted I would sometimes walk around at night, standing outside their houses, seeing below the doors the faint glow of dying embers and hearing an occasional laugh. Several of the families in our village had girls my age, but after beginning work in María's house, I rarely saw them.

My father had died of cholera years before, and my three sisters had all married and moved to other villages. They rarely visited our house. Augusto, my older brother, had a job as a bus driver's *ayudante*, and he had a room in the bus terminal in San Cristóbal. Occasionally he came home after a drinking spree in Cobán, and sometimes he left a pile of coins beside the candle on the altar in our front room. But my mother couldn't rely on him to take care of her, and every evening, cooking over a wood fire, she reminded me how important my job was. The work wasn't the kind a boy usually did, yet it was better than other jobs I might have had.

My full name is Pedro Antonio Rax Caal, although my classmates called me Pepe because my father had died and I was half an orphan. And on those rare occasions when I saw him, Augusto called me Ratón because I was small like a mouse and had tiny eyes. My mother called me Pedrito. In María's house, no one called me anything at all.

Even by the fourth day of work, I had not seen or heard María. I wanted to talk to my mother about her, but she had left to be with my sister Rosa in a village on the other side of the mountain. Rosa was expecting a baby.

I knew María was in the house. Every morning I began my work by removing the plate and cup from the table in the dining room. The plate and cup had traces of use: small bits of egg on the plate, a black ring of coffee at the bottom of the cup.

On Thursdays and Sundays I had to buy vegetables, fruit, and meat for María in the Santa Cruz market and put them in the refrigerator beside the sink in the kitchen. My mother said María had a voracious appetite—I noticed that on the fourth day, the day I brought more food, the refrigerator was empty—although I never saw any dirty pots and pans, only the plate and cup. And then there was her bathwater. After my wait downstairs, I returned to the bathroom to find María's bathwater suffused with sweet smells.

At the end of each day, I always listened outside María's bedroom. On the fifth day, I thought I heard someone sigh, but the sound could easily have been my own suppressed breathing.

On the sixth day, the house was still silent. Impatient and disturbed, I wanted to shout María's name. I thought of foolish acts—of walking into her bedroom or storming into her bath— but I needed to keep my job. It was all my family had. Every Sunday, a stack of bills, fresh and stiff, was waiting on the dining room table. When on the seventh day I picked up the money, I remembered again how important my job was to my mother.

María's silence, however, troubled me more every day. The house itself had become too familiar, and because I knew it so well, it seemed to have shrunk. My routine, boring initially, had become tedious. I thought only of María, and I expected to see her one day, sitting in the dining room or lounging on the couch, and I wondered if I would be able to contain my surprise, although I imagined she would act coolly, as if we had seen each other every day.

But I didn't see her, and her absence assumed its own presence in my life. I felt at times as if I were being stalked, and sometimes I would look up abruptly from my sweeping, thinking I had heard steps or a sniffle. On the ninth day, just before carrying the first pot of steaming water to her bath, I decided I wanted at least to hear María, and I knew I could do so if after I prepared her bathwater I simply waited in the library on the second floor.

With trembling hands, I dumped the first pot of hot water in the bath. I felt my mind was announcing my plan and that, thus informed, María was laughing silently in her bedroom. As I poured the last pot, I considered abandoning my scheme, suspecting that by now my nervous heart, the pounding of which seemed to reverberate off the bathroom walls, had given me away. But as I left the bathroom and beheld the silence again, the silence that seemed to encompass not only the house but the entire world, I resolved to carry on. I announced, "The bathwater's ready," then slipped into the library. I waited an hour, standing stiff and silent beside the bookcase, and heard nothing.

When I cleaned María's bath, I noticed it smelled stronger than it had on previous days, and not only of tangerines but of apples, which had come into season.

It took me a week to devise another plan. My first experience, however unsatisfying, had given me the confidence to proceed to the one place where I would, without a doubt, hear María: the bathroom closet. I was aware of the risks. I could make an inadvertent sound, a cough or hiccup. Worse was the possibility that María might have some business in the closet, open the door, and discover me.

Over the next week, I trained for my excursion. Because I would need to fit both myself and a pot into the closet (if I carried the last pot downstairs, then returned upstairs, I would give myself away) and because the closet was small and already contained a mop, I would have to stand in the pot. I spent my empty afternoon hours in the kitchen standing straight and silent in a pot. I held my position as long as I could. After three days of practice, I had no trouble standing in a pot for an hour.

I waited until Sunday, after I had picked my money off the dining room table. As soon as I told myself I was ready, I became nervous. I had survived my nervousness before during my previous attempt to hear María, but I knew this plan was far more dangerous. As hard as I tried, I couldn't keep my arms from moving in odd ways, like a chicken's wings batting the air. Sweat seeped from my forehead.

I considered abandoning my plan. But I badly wanted to hear María, and I was excited by my ingenuity. After tucking the pot into the bathroom closet, I stepped onto the landing and said, "The bathwater's ready." With the smoothness of a duck sliding across a pond, I slipped into the bathroom, stepped into the pot in the closet and gently shut the door.

I was calm; my mind had suppressed the beating of my heart. I was calm enough to hear everything: boys' delighted cries as they destroyed a piñata, a flock of birds descending into a tree. But as the minutes passed, I couldn't sustain my serenity. I felt the money, which I had divided and put into my two front pockets, squeeze against my thighs. I felt blood beat against my eyes and invade my extremities, knocking against my fingertips and toes. Before long, my entire body began to throb and I sweated, not small beads but giant drops that rolled off me like rain. I was sure María would hear my drops of sweat pelting the pot below me.

I tried to keep my equanimity, praying the hour had passed. But delirious from fear and sweat, I gave up. My head slammed against the door. The door opened and I fell on the floor.

I expected to hear a scream, but the only sound was of the door vibrating. I grabbed hold of it and stopped its trembling. Silence again. I celebrated the silence with deep breaths. I decided María hadn't bathed today. It was then, however, that I noticed the smell, thicker than at any fruit stand, a smell so sweet and powerful that my delirium, although a more pleasant variety, returned. I knew I had to resume my duties, but enveloped in María's smells, I felt paralyzed. I inhaled and inhaled again.

Groggy, I stood up. Twice I had to catch my balance against the wall, and when I bent to pick up the pot I nearly collapsed. The pot retrieved, I stumbled toward the door. My right foot caught against something soft, and when I looked down, I saw María's blouse. My heart rattled, but I calmed myself quickly, realizing that her clothes should be on the floor. I collected them and placed them in the pot. I walked to the door. The chain was strung across it.

I stood absolutely still, my heart raging against my chest. A minute or two passed before I was calm enough to reach up to unhook the chain. I took the knob between my thumb and forefinger and drew it delicately across the slide. I lifted it away from the release and lowered the chain carefully to the side of the door. I gripped the doorknob. Slowly, I turned it.

"*Haj nawojic?*" a voice said.

I didn't reply. I closed my eyes, praying that I had imagined the voice, soft and female. The voice spoke Pokomchí, and because of this, I decided the voice couldn't be María's. María was a Cakchiquel, and the Cakchiquels had their own language. I waited a long time in front of the door. I waited long enough to convince myself that I had imagined the voice.

I turned the knob again.

"*Haj nawojic?*"

I hunted for words, excuses. I thought of telling her that I had knocked myself out after some mishap with the pot and had fallen asleep in the closet. But even drunk on the rich smells of her bath, I recognized how implausible this would seem. I said nothing, too afraid to speak. I wondered if I should run.

"*Haj nawojic?*"

"*Pan kajen,*" I mumbled. Downstairs. The truth was all I could think to say.

She laughed, and her laughter troubled me. Was this the beginning of a cruel dismissal or had she found some humor in my aborted flight?

"*Re'hin yowab,*" I said. And I was sick. The sweet smells from her bath coupled with my anxiety made me want to vomit. I prayed for leniency.

She didn't respond for a long time, and I wondered if her silence was a signal to leave. I did not, however, want to make María angrier than she was.

"*Tengo una pistola,*" María said, her Spanish hard-sounding. "If you open the curtain in front of my bathtub, I'll blow off your face. Do you understand?"

"Yes," I said.

"Sit down," María said.

"Excuse me?"

"You heard me."

I slumped against the wall.

There was a long silence, and I began to wonder if I had imagined the entire conversation, the fruit smells making me hallucinate.

But she spoke again: "Why were you in my closet?"

I couldn't think of a convincing lie. "I wanted to hear you."

"Isn't the money I pay you sufficient?"

"Yes," I said.

"And the work isn't too hard, is it?"

"No."

"That's not enough?"

I didn't reply.

"It was enough for your mother, but it's not for you?"

I thought this might be María's way of firing me, a slow torture before she sent me trudging up the mountain to disgrace and poverty.

"I'm sorry," I said.

"Too late, *muchacho*, too late."

Again, I had nothing to say, and I thought it would be best for me to leave, to leave, that is, before I began to cry.

"How are you going to make up for what you've done?"

I thought about this. "I don't understand."

"You've broken the contract. You were someplace you weren't supposed to be. What will you do to make amends?"

I thought for a while. "I could clean the house again."

María laughed. "You just cleaned it, *muchacho*. Any other ideas?"

Nothing came to me for a long time, but then I thought about the *azadones*, rakes, and shovels in the room downstairs. "I could plant you a garden," I said.

"I've never had a garden. That would be nice, wouldn't it? You could plant carrots and radishes and celery. You could even plant me an apple tree, couldn't you?"

"Yes, I could," I said, seeing my salvation.

"But I won't have enough time," María said. "Not here, anyway. Carrots and celery take months. The earliest crop you could have for me is radishes, isn't it? Thirty days, right? I might not have thirty days."

"Thirty days isn't a long time," I pleaded. "It's just the right time now to plant radishes, and I'd bet they'd come up big and hot."

"Thirty days is a very long time," María said. "But we might make it. Yes, plant me some radishes tomorrow. Go to the *agropecuaría* in Santa Cruz this afternoon and tell them the woman in the white house on the highway needs some radish seeds. Yes, you can plant a radish garden."

"I'll plant it early tomorrow," I said, relieved.

"But what else?" she said. "That's too easy a punishment. I want you to think of something you can do now, right here, while you're sitting on the floor."

I thought a long time, too long. I heard the world expressing itself outside the house, the wind and the birds.

"Well?" she said.

I remembered what I did from time to time for my mother when she was tired or ill. I sat in a chair next to her bed and sang. The songs were in Spanish, although my mother spoke hardly any Spanish. I'd heard them on the radio and memorized them, and I knew that although my voice was weak, it soothed my mother, even if she didn't understand the words, and it was all I had now. So I sang for María, and the song ended:

> And then she robbed my heart
> Plundered it of its gold
> And she is still beautiful
> And I, alas, am old.

"All right," María said, laughing a little. "Not great, not even good, really, but all right. The song is stupid, but all right, you've made it today. This was only the first part of the test, and tomorrow you'll have to plant the radishes. After all, your crime was horrible. I'm going to leave now, so take your pot and return downstairs. Tomorrow, wait in the closet and I'll let you know when to come out. I want to hear about the radishes. Go now. Go. And practice, will you? Practice your singing. You sound like a mouse."

The next morning, I began my act of contrition by making María a garden. I used the *azadón* from the toolroom and dug up a patch of grass in the backyard. The roots of the grass grew deep, and I had to swing the *azadón* hard to cut deep enough to reach the ends of the roots. It was difficult to pull up the earth, as if some fierce animal, hidden in the ground, had its jaws around the blade. I carved a square patch of dirt, my face hot and my arms aching. In the middle of the patch, I made a mound of dirt as tall as my waist. I chopped at the mound with a machete, slicing the balls of dirt into smaller balls and then into smooth soil. When the entire mound had become soil, I shaped it into a long, wide bed. I carved three trenches in the bed with the handle of my *azadón*. Then I sprinkled the seeds into the trenches. When I was done planting, I swept a light covering of soil over the seeds.

After María summoned me from the bathroom closet, she asked

about the garden. I told her proudly about planting the radish seeds. There was silence, and I thought she might be deciding on some appropriate response, some words of praise for my work.

"A house should be like a garden, shouldn't it?" María said. "Full of life. Everything growing. Children, I mean. But this house isn't much like a garden, is it? What's it like?"

"It's a house," I said, disappointed.

"No, tell me what it's like. If it isn't like a garden, it has to be like something else. Not what it is, but what it's like."

I thought hard but couldn't think of anything to say.

"Well, I was thinking it might be like a cemetery. Very quiet. Señor Prado would like it to be a garden, of course. Even though he already has three children with his wife and seven more children with two other women, he wants children with me."

She laughed. "Why not? He has enough money. Do you know how much money Señor Prado has?"

"No."

"Two hundred million," she said. "Two hundred million United States dollars."

I whistled.

"He could support a whole town full of children," she said. "At one time, he thought I wanted his children. He thought I was sad when I didn't have a child with him. He thinks all women want children. He may be right, but all women don't want *his* children."

She paused. "Thank you for the garden," she said. "I'm happy. Now sing for me. Sing a song about a woman who becomes a bird."

"I'm sorry, I don't know a song like that."

"Invent it," she said. "Write me a song about a woman who becomes a bird or I'll shoot you." She laughed, long and sweet, and then told me to leave the bathroom.

My mother had warned me about the helicopter and the way it sounded. She said you could hear the helicopter from a long way, the sound at first like a dog's growl. Growing nearer, it sounded like a swarm of bees. Nearer still, it sounded like nothing natural, like some invasion from the sky. The house shook as in an earthquake, and you felt the world was about to be destroyed.

Señor Prado's helicopter descended the next day, rattling the house before landing behind the high wall in the front yard. His two bodyguards stepped off; Señor Prado followed. He was a heavy man with black hair speckled with white. My mother had warned me not to look at Señor Prado, but standing at the dining room window, I watched him as he walked to the front door. When I saw the handle turn, I raced to the kitchen.

As I put the pots of water on the stove, I heard Señor Prado walk into the adjacent room, his study, and fall into his cushioned chair, the displaced air escaping like a long sigh. The water was lukewarm when I heard Señor Prado leave his chair and walk up the stairs to María's bedroom. The water had been boiling for several minutes when I heard him open the bedroom door and yell, "Hot water!"

After his bath with María, Señor Prado returned to his study. I wasn't supposed to come near him, so I walked from the kitchen into the living room, then up the stairs. I cleaned the bathtub, which did not smell like fruits, as when María bathed alone, but like plants that grow beside rivers, a strong and bitter smell. When I finished cleaning the bathtub, I heeded my mother's advice and stayed away from Señor Prado. I worked on the second floor, dusting the bookshelf, peering out the library window occasionally to observe Señor Prado's bodyguards marching side by side around the house in the rain.

But I couldn't sustain my indifference. It was exciting to know someone else was in the house whom I could actually see. Certain I could be invisible, I abandoned the second floor, slipped noiselessly into the kitchen, and crouched outside the entrance to his study. Cautiously, I peered in. With glasses perched like giant fish eyes on top of his nose, Señor Prado was reading a white leather book. A stack of similar books was on the white bookshelf behind him. Presently, he cleared his throat and read aloud:

"On the fifteenth of that month, I celebrated my fifteenth birthday. This was the first birthday I had spent without my father, who had died the year before in a machete fight with a neighbor."

I withdrew my face and sat next to the door, listening to his strong, vibrant voice.

"My brother Mauricio acted as my guide to manhood and took me to a whorehouse that night. I don't remember too much about the place, only that it smelled faintly of urine and strongly of beer. I remember the woman who served us. She was wearing a dress that looked like it was made of rose petals, and of course it was as tight as a pair of hands strangling a neck. My brother seemed to be in love with her, repeating a thousand times 'mi amor,' the only term of affection he could remember after his sixth beer. He appeared to have forgotten the purpose of our visit. When he began his seventh beer, I slipped off my stool and out of the whorehouse. I had a feeling my true adventure was about to begin.

"I walked into the night under a great covering of stars, and I heard a familiar voice. My friend Omar was calling me. Together we walked toward the desert, where we often hunted snakes. It was a clear night, the clearest I'd ever seen, and it was obvious, at least to me, that we would find no snakes that night, with the desert spread out before us bright and empty. We soon gave up hunting and by silent agreement walked west toward the river.

"The river, this beautiful and curving thing slinking through the driest part of the country, must have been quite a sight to the people who passed our parched town on their way to some richer place. But to us the river was no more remarkable than the basketball court, which in the dry season filled with enough dust to plant corn on, or the church, built in the sixteenth century, that looked over our town like a giant angel.

"Omar and I expected the river to be deserted. After all, it was past one in the morning, late enough for some of the cantinas to be closing. Whispering—it seemed appropriate to whisper, as if spirits were nearby—we decided to bathe. We stripped to our underwear, but just as we were about to enter the river, we heard a voice.

"It was a female voice, high and clear and a little mournful. We debated where the voice was coming from; I thought the north and Omar said the south. We decided to split up, each of us to explore our preferred territory, and meet in half an hour. We put on our clothes and parted.

"I marched above the riverbank, following the voice, which at times seemed to draw near, although just when it grew strongest, it would fade, and I would give up hope. I wondered if the voice were coming from some cowboy's radio deep in the desert. But as I was about to turn back, I saw her. She was standing in the middle of the river, the water up to her waist. She had no blouse on, and her breasts were large and round. She was not cast in white, like everything else the moonlight touched, but seemed golden, as if a lamp were burning within her. She was not singing, exactly, not speaking. I couldn't understand the words she recited, although they seemed like some kind of prayer.

"I crouched, but I knew I was visible. My presence, however, did not seem to bother her. Rather, it seemed to encourage her; her voice became higher, sweeter, more melodic. I wondered if she were calling me, and I knew any man worth his name would approach her to see what she wanted. But I was frozen in the desert.

"I heard footsteps behind me. I'd forgotten Omar. 'I saw her,' he said. 'She's down here. Come on.' I looked at him, puzzled. 'No,' I said, 'she's right here.' I pointed to the river, but the woman was gone."

Feeling disappointed for Señor Prado, I sighed.

"Devil, what?" I heard Señor Prado call. I flinched, my heart thundering against my chest. Pistol shots splattered the kitchen, puncturing the blue pots hanging on the far wall. I wet my pants.

When the shots stopped, Señor Prado said, "Come here slowly and with your hands up."

Shivering in shame and fear, I didn't respond.

"I know you're in there—I heard you sigh—and I'll come after you if you want to play that way. I love hunting, and I'm very good at it. Haven't you seen the jaguar? I shot it from fifty meters. You'd be a much easier target. So it'd be better if you came forward now. I can't promise that I won't kill you, but I will promise you death if I have to chase you."

I stood and marched into his study with my hands held high and my pants streaked with urine. He removed his boot and shoved his hand into it. "Devil," he said. "I can never find my other pistol. There, is that it? No? Right, right, it must be in the other boot." He looked at me and smiled, and I breathed easier. "Give me a second, will you?"

"Yes, señor."

He removed his other boot and put his hand inside. "There it is." He pulled out a tiny silver pistol, which he pointed at me. "You should have run," he said.

"I'm sorry, señor."

"Sorry for not running?"

"No, señor, not for that."

"For listening while I was reading?"

"Yes, señor."

"You should be sorry. And I should kill you. But I'm too old and blind. My glasses fell to the floor when I shot at you. You see, I can't even see which way my pistol is facing. Is it facing you or me?"

"Me, señor."

"How can I be sure? You might be lying, you see, and then if I do decide to shoot you I might end up shooting myself."

"Yes, señor."

"But neither of us need be afraid because I can't get my finger on the trigger anyway. My finger is too swollen and this pistol is too small and, anyway, you should run now if you're going to run."

"I'm not going to run, señor."

"All right, fine. Good. Tell me, then, who are you?"

"I'm the boy who cleans the house."

"Right, right. Well, it's a pleasure and all that, now get back to work."

"Yes, señor." I turned to leave.

"Wait a second, just a second," Señor Prado said. "I need you to find my glasses."

I walked swiftly to his side. "Not so fast," he said, pointing the pistol at me. I jumped back.

"Sorry," he said, "if you could just do things a little more gracefully, it would be helpful. Pretend you're doing ballet. Have you ever seen ballet?"

"No, señor."

"Well, then very slowly, always do things very slowly around me, please."

I bent down as slowly as I could to pick up the fish-eye glasses. "Yes," he said when I'd handed them to him. "That's exactly right. Yes, indeed. You've done well. Now, go back to work and don't watch me anymore. Next time I *will* kill you."

I walked toward the kitchen. "Wait," he called. "One more question."

"Yes señor?"

"Do you like my memoirs?"

"Excuse me, señor?"

"My memoirs. The story I just read for you."

"Oh, yes, I do, señor. Yes I do."

Later, after Señor Prado had left in his helicopter, I wondered about the last thing he'd told me, how he'd phrased it: 'The story I just read for you.'

The next morning, María called me in from the closet, and I sat on the floor, inhaling the fruit-stand smells of her bath in front of the closed curtain.

"Did you write the song I asked for?"

"Yes."

"Let's hear it."

I sang for her, my voice sounding hollow against the bathroom walls.

"I see," María said before I'd finished. "'Beautiful woman with light in her eyes flies free toward bright blue skies.' In songs it's always beautiful women, isn't it?"

I waited for her to say something more. The song, though short, had taken me several hours to write. Singing it to myself on my way to María's house, I had imagined María praising it—no, more—falling in love with the song and the singer.

"Am I beautiful?" María asked.

"Yes," I said gallantly.

María laughed. "*Tonto*," she said. "Idiot. You don't know."

"No," I admitted.

"And you won't know until you're ready. You must first know me, then you'll see me. Understand?"

"Yes."

"Then I'll begin with my history: My mother was a beekeeper. She learned from her own mother. This was something the women in my mother's family did.

"We lived in a three-room adobe house on a coffee *finca*. I had three older brothers. They worked on the *finca* with my father. I stayed home with my mother. She cooked and cleaned, of course, did all the jobs a woman is supposed to do. But she also tended her bees. My grandmother and great-grandmother used logs as hives, closing the ends with clay or stone. My mother used some logs, though she also built drawers from wood and at harvest would remove the drawers and strain the honey through a *cedazo*. My mother and grandmother and great-grandmother worked with stingless bees, and stingless bees are supposed to produce less honey, but our buckets were always full. My mother sold her honey to the people on the *finca*.

"She had books on how to tend bees. Some of the books were in Spanish, new manuals she ordered from a store in Cobán, but she also had old notebooks with dusty pages that her mother and grandmother and great-grandmother had drawn on, pictures showing how much honey was produced in a certain year, how eucalyptus trees could be planted nearby to increase the production, and, especially, very pretty sketches of the queen bee.

"I learned from my mother how to make and harvest honey. When I carried honeycombs, I felt like I was carrying gold. I spent several years working with my mother as a beekeeper, and I sat beside her at night as she wrote in new notebooks. She'd learned to write in Cakchiquel—it was for so long only an oral language, but someone had finally written down the words and she'd gotten hold of a dictionary. When I was fifteen, she allowed me to keep my own notebooks on what I'd seen and done with the bees. Then the manager of the *finca*, Don Rafael, told my father he thought I would make an excellent candidate for the Rabin Ajau pageant. Don Rafael said he would buy me a new *traje*, to look beautiful, and my father agreed. And so I became a candidate for queen of the *indígenas*. This, I thought, would be wonderful. I wanted to be a queen, like the queen bee. And this is where I met Señor Prado. And I never again tended bees. And here I am in this house. A queen in this house."

She laughed, short and sharp. "I'm a queen," she said.

With my mother gone, I had to fix my own meals. Sometimes I'd build a fire and boil eggs and eat raw carrots. Sometimes I was too tired to cook, and I would fall into bed and begin dreaming instantly. In my dreams, María would rise up from my exhaustion to greet me behind a curtain of steam. Sometimes she looked like my mother and sometimes like one of my sisters and sometimes like Señor Prado's woman in the river—large breasted and glowing.

One night, I was asleep when Augusto came home, half-drunk and singing. I opened my eyes and saw him standing across the room. He had a pistol in his hand, and I thought he was going to kill me. This was brief, unfounded panic, and it passed quickly.

Later, waking from a dream, I saw him slumped in a chair, and I thought he was Señor Prado. I didn't know if I should be scared or grateful. Then I realized the man across the room was my brother, and I slept again.

"I'll tell you who the suspects are in the murder," María said after I'd come from her closet and sat beside her curtained tub, "and you tell me who killed him, all right?"

"The murder?" I asked.

"Yes, the murder of Señor Prado."

"Did someone kill Señor Prado?"

"Yes," María said.

"When?" I asked, amazed.

"I don't know exactly when, since it hasn't happened yet. But it will happen. I know. He knows too. Now, I'll tell you the suspects and you guess who killed him, all right?"

"All right."

"Suspect number one," María said, "is his former business partner, Ricardo Asturias. Señor Asturias comes from one of the country's wealthiest families. He's a little older than Señor Prado, and because of his age and social status, he once saw himself as Señor Prado's mentor.

"Señor Prado, I should tell you, doesn't come from a wealthy family. He was born to a poor mother—a Chortí indígena— in the Chiquimula desert, and he never went to school. But he worked hard, first as a bus driver's ayudante, then as a bus driver. Before he was twenty-five, he owned the bus company. After he bought the other three bus lines in the eastern part of the country, it was only natural that he merge with Señor Asturias, who owned the bus lines in the west, and that together they buy the northern and southern bus lines.

"Señor Asturias didn't like Señor Prado's idea of buying the national airline company. Too expensive, he said. Too many crashes. So with his own money, Señor Prado bought the airline, and he made three times as much money as he did on the buses. Before long he had enough money to buy Señor Asturias's share in the bus companies.

"All Señor Asturias's friends laughed at him and said Señor Prado had made him look like a fool. It's not wise to make a rich man look like a fool, even if you're rich yourself.

"Suspect number two is a mysterious man, one of the biggest drug lords in this part of the world. No one knows his name, and he looks different depending on who you talk to. One thing is certain, though: he's rich and dangerous.

"However, he's been getting a little competition lately. Not long ago, several of the men who worked for him deserted him for another mysterious man. This second mysterious man—who both you and I know—gives these men a larger share of the profits, and they like this very much. The first mysterious man isn't used to competition, so he's furious. He's been hunting this second mysterious man, and if he finds him unguarded, he'll kill him.

"The third suspect is Doña Alicia Fernández de Prado, Señor Prado's wife. She's an old woman who likes roses, even though her little hands are far too delicate to tend her own garden. Of course, she hasn't had to use her hands for anything since she married Señor Prado.

"She's known all along about his mistresses, but she feels especially threatened by his *indígena* mistress. Señor Prado doesn't spend much time with me—only one or two days a month—but all the same his wife senses his obsession; and it's only grown in the seven years I've lived in this house. She's afraid Señor Prado will leave me his entire fortune, though she knows he hasn't rewritten his will yet.

"A month ago, she confronted Señor Prado. She cried and ranted and pleaded. Señor Prado left me to play the dutiful husband. He consoled her as they drank *limonada* and watched their dozen gardeners trim the rosebushes. After a month, Señor Prado returned to me.

"Señora Prado doesn't know how to use a gun herself, and she wouldn't have the stomach for murder anyway. But she's quite capable of hiring someone to do the job. Señor Prado has been very generous to his wife, generous enough to pay for his own assassination.

"An entire country is our fourth suspect, the most powerful country in the world, the United States of America. A lot of people believe Señor Prado is going to run for president next year, and though he isn't famous now, not in all parts of the country anyway, he has enough money to become famous very fast. The government of the United States doesn't want Señor Prado to run for president. The government of the United States doesn't like foreign leaders who sell drugs. They had enough trouble with Señor Noriega in Panama. To prevent a similar situation, they might eliminate Señor Prado sooner rather than later.

"The fifth suspect is the guerrillas. As you know, the guerrillas aren't fond of rich men, especially rich *ladino* men like Señor Prado, even if his mother was a Chortí. Señor Prado owns several coffee plantations in this part of the country—he bought them after he got bored with his busses and airplanes—but he pays his workers very little, and the guerrillas don't like this. So you see, the guerrillas would be very pleased to kill another exploiter of the masses.

"The sixth suspect is the army. Yes, the army. It might seem odd that the guerrillas and the army would want to kill the same man, but wars have never been logical. Although Señor Prado pays his workers very little, he recently started giving them a few centavos more than the usual wage, and workers at other plantations heard about it and are unhappy with what they're earning. Señor Prado's fellow plantation owners hate the unrest, and they may turn to their friends in the army to eliminate the source of their problem.

"Now, the seventh suspect. Well, that would have to be me, although I'm not a very likely one. On the surface, I don't have a lot to gain from Señor Prado's death. This house won't be mine when he dies; Señor Prado has made it clear to me that he'll leave me nothing unless I have his child. Besides, I'm only a weak little *indígena* girl.

"But maybe I'm not interested in the house. Maybe I'd kill him because, while I have everything a person needs to live, I don't have a life. Maybe I'd kill him because he took me away from my home and tried to steal my *costumbre*. You've seen that he buys me only blue jeans and black blouses. And he won't let me leave the house. He told me about the contract he has with some men in town. If they see me outside the house, they'll kill me. They'll be rich men if they find me outside.

"And maybe I'd kill him because I'd found another lover, a lover perhaps not as old as I, but someone who shares my blood." She laughed. "How old are you?"

"Sixteen," I said.

"I'm twenty-four. You see?"

There was a pause, then she laughed again.

"Should I add your name?" she asked.

"I don't understand."

"As a suspect."

"But why would I kill Señor Prado?"

"Because you love me. Or you will. Before he dies."

After María's revelations, it was hard to continue working as I had been. Around every corner of the house, I expected to see some gun-bearing monster. My dread grew darker with the day, and by the afternoon I imagined all seven suspects gathered in the living room, weapons hanging from their necks like rosaries. The leader of the group was María, her hair long and black and her face round and radiant like a brown sun. In my vision, she held no weapon but wore a *güipil* as red as blood. The other assassins waited on her word. Kill.

Yet walking home through the light embrace of the forest at the end of the day, I wondered if she were joking, playing on my ignorance. If Señor Prado were in as much danger as she said, why would María's house have only the front wall guarding it? Anyone could come from the forest behind the house—the backyard had no wall—and beat down the backdoor.

But my fear and perplexity did not curb my rising passion. Standing the next day in the bathroom closet, I imagined myself singing for María while the two of us bathed. I felt I could make the house tremble with my song. I could be an earthquake or a helicopter.

"*Okinik,*" María said.

I opened the door, although as I did so I realized I didn't know what she'd said. She wasn't speaking Pokomchí.

"I said, 'Come in,'" María said, as if anticipating my question. "This is my language. This is Cakchiquel."

"It's strange."

"Yes, it's different from Pokomchí. To think that some of our villages even touch, that in one cornfield a farmer speaks Pokomchí and in the field next to it he speaks Cakchiquel."

This was true. In the village below ours, the people spoke only Cakchiquel. We never spoke with them.

"I know a little Pokomchí, thanks to your mother. She didn't like to talk with me, but often I'd hear her talking to herself, and I'd ask her to explain what she was saying. She was always embarrassed. I don't know why. I talk to myself too. It's what you have to do in this house." María laughed.

"There are twenty-two Maya languages in our country. Imagine. We're all the same people, but we can't understand each other. When I was at the Rabin Ajau, all the candidates were gathered in a room under the stage. We were dressing, admiring each other's *trajes,* when someone said, 'We're all speaking Spanish.' This was obvious, but not so obvious. Here we were, all *indígena* girls—all of us with our own Maya languages, and all of us speaking Spanish." María paused. "What do you know about our history?"

I'd studied about the old Maya civilization in El Instituto Básico. I'd even read the *Popul Vuh.* But I wanted to hear what María would say. "Nothing."

"In ancient times," she said, "we Mayas had a more accurate calendar than the Europeans. We had a way to predict eclipses. We had whole libraries, books about mathematics and philosophy and astronomy. But the Spanish destroyed our libraries and burned our books. And they murdered our people, demolished our empire. So here we were at the pageant, putting on our pretty *indígena* clothes to parade in front of the descendants of people who had ruined our culture, and the only way we could communicate with each other was to speak their language.

"The girl who made the comment about us all speaking Spanish walked to the middle of the room. We formed a large circle around her. What a circle, what color. She said, 'Ch'ona,' which in her language, Kekchí, is the way to say hello to a woman. And we responded with the same greeting.

"She said, 'Chan xacuil?' This means 'How are you?' She told us how to respond. 'Mac'a'. Jo'xak a'in.' 'Fine, as you see.' And we repeated this exchange three or four times until we learned it. And you should have heard the way the room sounded the last time we repeated it. We were shouting like we'd won a war.

"Another girl stepped in the center of the circle and spoke some of her language and we learned the phrases she spoke. We shouted them like we wanted God to hear.

"One of the men who was running the pageant came down. He was a light-skinned man with red hair. He said that we needed to be quiet because the people were arriving and some had complained about the noise coming from below their feet.

"We laughed at the man. Yes, we laughed. We cursed him in our languages. We covered him with our curses. When he left, we laughed again, a laughter that was like a song. But then there was silence. I'm sure everyone was thinking about the pageant and how they could win. We had to go and look beautiful in front of all those men in suits and women in long dresses and high-heeled shoes. And we wanted to win. All of us. Why?"

"And you won," I said.

"No, I didn't win. I got second place. The girl who won was prettier than I was. I'm sure Señor Prado fell in love with her first. But she was very busy because she was queen of the indigenous people. She met President García, and a few months after the pageant she flew to the United States, to California, to march in a parade with many roses. She met an American athlete—a football player—and they fell in love without language and she stayed in the United States. Señor Prado showed me the newspaper article. He cut the picture out and put it on the wall in the dining room. You've seen the pictures on the wall, haven't you?"

"Yes."

"Those are all *indígena* brides who didn't marry *indígena* men.

Most of them married *ladinos*. Some married gringos. Señor Prado likes to call it the Wall of Lost Voices. He thinks that because they've married *ladinos* or *gringos* they've sold their souls. And maybe they have. How many of those girls will speak *indígena* languages to their children?

"And—look—you and I are speaking Spanish and our blood is Maya. I know some of your language, but you need to know some of mine. I'll teach you."

I learned how to say Hello, how to ask 'How are you?' I learned how to say water and bath.

"*Qate'*," María said. "Our mother."

"*Qate'*," I repeated.

"*Qatata'*," she said. "Our father."

"*Qatata'*."

"*Qakik'el*," she said. "Our blood."

Facing the mountain at the end of the day, I imagined myself charging up it, a warrior in battle, ready to die. I was prepared to give my life to restore the kingdom, to make María queen. It was a beautiful thought: to die for María.

When I reached the top of the mountain, I stared down at the highway and saw a red car race around a few curves, then hit a long, straight stretch in front of María's house. The car shot by, then slid into another curve, then disappeared. Even before I'd ever seen cars, I'd heard people speak of them in my village. I envisioned them as metal horses, and when I finally saw one, I was impressed with its sheen and color but disappointed that it lacked a horse's fiery eyes and flaring black nose.

Staring at the darkening highway, I remembered that it was the Spanish who brought the horse to our world. Horses and cars— all foreign. On my side, I had only my feet to plant firm in the ground, to defend the mountain from forces rising from below.

Teasingly, María called me *metz*, what lovers call each other in Pokomchí. When I sang her another song I wrote about a poor girl who becomes a princess, she said, "I have a *metz* who invents songs for me. I am a lucky girl."

She asked me about the garden, and I told her the leaves of the radishes were becoming thick and green, and she asked when the radishes would be ready. I told her in two weeks, and she said, "Excellent," but she did not want to talk about the radishes. She wanted to talk about Señor Prado, and I listened, jealous and fascinated.

"Because Señor Prado is a rich man," María said, "he is invited to spend time with other rich men, who hope to make themselves richer with Señor Prado's money. Señor Prado isn't well-bred like these other men, whose parents or grandparents or great-grandparents were born in Spain or Belgium or Germany. But two hundred million U.S. dollars is enough to convince men who have European parents to spend a little time with the descendant of a Chortí.

"Señor Prado knows all the rich men in the country. There are so few of them. You've heard of Alejandro Carpio?"

The name sounded familiar, but I said I hadn't.

"He's one of the two wealthiest men in the country, wealthier than Señor Prado. He owns almost all the land in the Petén, and on his land, as an amusement, he has a zoo. It's an open zoo where the animals roam in large fields. People drive through and see jaguars, elephants, giraffes, even polar bears. I don't know how the polar bears stand the heat. But if Alejandro Carpio wants polar bears, he won't let heat stop him. He can pay a hundred *campesinos* to wave fans.

"Alejandro Carpio breeds his animals very successfully. It's like that with rich men. Whatever they touch seems to reproduce. Well, almost everything they touch." María laughed. "Anyway, he breeds too many of these animals for his zoo. So he allows other rich men to hunt them—for a fee, of course.

"Señor Prado was very interested in hunting Alejandro Carpio's animals, and when he offered enough money—twice the usual fee—it was arranged.

"Señor Prado arrived on a weekend that many of Alejandro Carpio's friends were present for a polo tournament. Before beginning the tournament, Alejandro Carpio wanted to take care of Señor Prado's hunt. He loaned Señor Prado his rifle and led him to the cage with a jaguar. Señor Prado requested a jaguar because it lives in our country. He could have killed a polar bear or a cheetah, but these are foreign animals and he didn't want to kill a foreign animal.

"The cage was no bigger than the living room downstairs. And Señor Prado stood outside of it with the rifle, aiming through the fence at the jaguar. Alejandro Carpio had to prod the jaguar before it moved. As you know, Señor Prado doesn't see well, and he spent many minutes tracking the jaguar, which was pacing at the back of the cage. Finally, he shot, but his aim was poor. The jaguar paced even faster. Señor Prado needed even more time to track the jaguar, but his shot missed again.

"Alejandro Carpio was impatient—all his friends were waiting—so he had a divider lowered into the cage, trapping the jaguar in a space about the size of this bathroom. Even Señor Prado couldn't miss. When the jaguar came within inches of his rifle, Señor Prado blew a hole in its neck.

"As Señor Prado was waiting for Alejandro Carpio's workers to stuff and mount the jaguar, one of Alejandro Carpio's friends rode up on his horse. He said to Señor Prado, 'Shine my boots, boy.' Señor Prado said, 'You must be mistaken.' The man said, 'Oh, so you're not the stable boy? You look just like a stable boy.' He laughed, and Señor Prado noticed Alejandro Carpio laughing too.

"Señor Prado told me this a long time ago, when he thought I might feel sorry for him. But I, too, laughed. He should know he can't buy lighter skin or a European mother.

"Maybe I'm too cruel. After all, he's been good to me. I live in this nice house. I eat well. Even my mind is nourished. I have the library, filled with books. Señor Prado brings me new books each month. I don't think he even looks at the books before he buys them. I have everything: a novel about an American girl who inherits a lot of money and marries an evil man; a biography of Nicholas II, the czar of Russia; even a book about how to build a sailboat. I read them all. He doesn't ask about them. He doesn't know what the books do. They make me hate him more, even the book about building a sailboat. I would like a sailboat, even if we are living in the mountains. Would you sail with me, *metz*?

"I know he considers the books part of the battle. They're in Spanish, and he must think all their words will drown out my own language. And the truth is, they have. I'm forgetting Cakchiquel. There's no one to speak with. Yesterday, for just a second, I couldn't remember the word for beautiful. I remembered it quickly, but for that second I was very scared. And now I wonder how much Cakchiquel I've forgotten. Sometimes I know a word in Spanish but I don't know it in my own language. And I wonder if it's because Cakchiquel doesn't have such a word or if I once knew it and I forgot. What is the word for beautiful in Pokomchí?"

"*Holohic*," I said.

"Then if I forget, it'll be my word, too. *Holohic*. And you must remember the word for beautiful in Cakchiquel. The word is *cha'omalaj*. Remember so that if one of us ever forgets, we'll have our word."

Señor Prado arrived the next day. After pouring the bathwater, I went to the toolroom, where I decided to remain until I heard Señor Prado leave in his helicopter. Señor Prado was my rival, and I didn't want to see him. Or I pretended I didn't. Yes, I was jealous of his relationship with María—how casually he could come and go, how casually he could enter her bedroom and bath. But I felt a kinship with him, too, because he had what I wanted. And he seemed to like me, despite his odd behavior with pistols. He seemed to like me because he had read me his story.

When one of his bodyguards walked in from the backdoor and said, "Señor Prado would like you to listen where you were listening before," I couldn't help myself: rival or no, I was delighted. I walked into the kitchen and sat by the door of Señor Prado's study.

Señor Prado opened the book and cleared his throat. "Ready?" he asked.

"Yes!" I said, with shameful glee.

He began: "I looked for the woman on other nights. She became not just an obsession but a spirit that inhabited my body. I could feel her in the blood that danced out of my heart. I thought of her always, wherever I was. I heard her voice in every voice on the radio. I saw her on every street corner, in front of every store. I dreamed of her at night, and when I woke I did not stop dreaming of her.

"I ventured alone through the desert, to the river, waiting patiently in the same spot where I'd seen her. I listened and heard sounds I never imagined existed: snakes whistling, vultures snoring, cattle laughing. I heard the earth itself, its creaks and groans. But I didn't hear what I wanted to hear.

"Some nights I waited with Omar, and I watched him fall asleep and heard his heavy breathing mix with the other night sounds. One night I made Omar go to where he had seen his woman while I waited for mine, and Omar trudged through the sand only to return ten minutes later, near tears, telling me he didn't want to be alone—I had frightened him with my story about the woman—and besides, he had been lying the other time, he had never seen a woman. I told him it didn't matter; it only mattered that he stood exactly where he'd stood before. If he did this, perhaps we would again be in harmony with the desert and my woman would return. Omar walked back into the darkness, but my woman didn't appear.

"I didn't forget her. But time tempers even maniacal obsessions, and she was beginning to escape me slowly, like blood from a wound. I began to notice that the women I mistook for her on the streets were not at all unattractive, and I even ventured to talk with one or two, although I was too young and too poor to interest them much.

"She must have known about my infidelity and conjured up another night as clear as the first. The night was so gloriously bright that the men from the town left their houses at midnight, as if summoned, and played soccer under the stars. I didn't follow everyone in town to the stadium but raced as fast as I could to the river. As I approached, I heard her voice above the crunch of my feet. I dashed to the river's edge and saw her, midstream, her chest glowing as if gold were set ablaze within her.

"She turned to me. There was nothing in her face to detain me; her face was as welcome and warm as the light that radiated from her chest. But I hesitated. I was not, I'll admit, a good swimmer, and I worried about the water and its depth. I was concerned the current might be too strong, that I might be swept away before I could reach her, and that this would put her in the position of either saving me or laughing as I was swept downstream. I hesitated. I did not hesitate long, but it was too long. She frowned. I ran into the water and began a horrible crawl toward her.

"The current was strong, and I fought it, pounding it with my fists, slapping it with my feet. I propelled my body through the cold water with the force of my desire. I drank water and I felt I could drink the entire river, could suck it all into my gut if it was what I must do to have her.

"This feeling did not last long. I was soon choking, and I was afraid I was about to die. I struggled toward the surface, thrashing madly as if trying to escape someone's grip. I gave up. I lifted my arms, my last plea, and sank.

"A few seconds later, however, my feet struck mud, and when I made my body erect, I found that I could stand and breathe. My chin was under water but my lips were above it. I concentrated on sucking up the hot air; my panic subsided. It was only when I conceded that I was no longer drowning that I looked for her. I spun around, scanning the water, the shore. She was gone."

I heard Señor Prado shut his book. "Well?" Señor Prado said. "What do you think?"

"It's beautiful," I said, "and sad."

Señor Prado sighed. "Yes, exactly." He paused. "Step in here," he said.

I walked into his study.

Señor Prado squinted at me through his mammoth glasses. "Don't come any nearer, please. I don't want to shoot you." He pulled his pistol from his pocket and waved it at me. "Describe yourself."

"Señor?"

"Tell me who you are."

"I'm the boy who cleans the house."

"No, who are you really?"

"Excuse me, señor, I don't know what you mean."

"Exactly," Señor Prado said. "Exactly." He put his pistol down. "Someday you'll know."

I thinned the radish garden, pulling up the weaker plants. Even these smelled sharp. I cleaned a tiny radish in the kitchen sink and bit into it, but it was too bitter and I spat it back.

In María's closet, I crouched and pressed my ear against the door. I had learned to suppress my heart; it was as still as a pond. I waited to hear the bathroom door open. I waited to hear her footsteps. I waited to hear her sweep aside the bathroom curtain. I waited and heard nothing until María said "*Okinik.*"

I took my place on the floor, perplexed by her soundlessness but pleased, as always, to be with her.

"I have a new song," I announced proudly.

"Not another song about a beautiful woman?" María said.

It was, and I admitted so reluctantly.

"You need to close your eyes and listen," she said. "But even blind men want to tell women they're beautiful. Señor Prado calls me beautiful even though from a meter away he can't tell what color earrings I have on or even if I'm wearing earrings. And he's old, you know, even older than he looks. He used to do what men like to do." She laughed. "Now he only likes to tell me stories. Oh, he's wonderful at telling stories. Listening to him, you can close your eyes and pretend you're dreaming."

I knew, of course, about his stories. But I didn't want her to be as fascinated with them as I was. I wanted her to love my singing above all, to request my songs, long for them and me.

"He hasn't touched me in a year, even when we're in the bathtub together. He sits at one end and I sit at the other. I don't even feel his feet. He starts telling a story as soon as he steps in. I don't know. Maybe he and his wife are, you know, more intimate now, so he doesn't need it from me." She laughed again, a little sadly. "He doesn't tell me much about what goes on in his life, only to say that he'll be killed soon. And I've heard all about that. No, he tells me stories about when he was an infant."

"He's writing a book," I said, "about his life."

"How do you know?"

"He read me some of it."

"Well. Now he's telling you stories too."

"He has a lot of white books downstairs. They're full of his writing. He read to me from one of the books."

"I never go into Señor Prado's study. He made it very clear to me that if I stepped foot in that study, he'd kill me. Of course, he always uses that threat. But in this case, I think he's serious. He told me about one of his mistresses who, well . . ."

"What?"

"Well, she was punished, you could say, for being too inquisitive."

"What do you mean?" I asked.

María didn't answer, and what she said next distracted me, amazed me: "Would you like to touch me?"

"Excuse me?"

"You heard me."

I badly wanted to touch her, but I hadn't even seen her. I sensed a trick.

"The last time Señor Prado was here I asked him if he'd like to touch me," she said. "He told me a story about when he was seven years old and he and his family went to Esquipulas to visit the statue of the Black Christ. He was a short boy and he could only reach Christ's toes." She giggled. "That was his story about touching. Yes, he does tell funny stories." She sighed.

"You could begin to touch me," she said, "by taking a bath in my water. Would you like that?"

"Yes."

"Good. You may use my water. Now go to your closet, whisper my name thirty times, then come out."

I entered the closet and spoke María's name thirty times with the urgency of a prayer. Finished, I opened the closet door and approached the curtain guarding the bath. For a moment, I imagined María behind it, and the thought made my heart pound. When I pulled aside the curtain, the bathtub was empty. It smelled like a collision of watermelons, cherries, apples, strawberries, and cantaloupes, and the smell stormed my nostrils like flames. I sat on the edge of the bath and placed my hand in the water, which seemed as hot as when I had hauled it up the stairs. I moved my hand back and forth, stirring up another smell, a deep smell, stronger than the others. This smell filled my lungs, and when I opened my mouth I could taste it. I chewed it, sucked it, licked it. I felt it deep in my gut, warm in my stomach.

I took off my shoes, socks, and shirt. I looked around, thinking María might be somewhere, watching me. I even opened the closet door to see if María had decided to play the same trick I'd played on her, but the closet was empty.

I removed my pants. Not trusting the silence, however, I kept my underpants on.

When I stepped into her bath, my feet slid along the bottom as if in mud and I plunged backward into the water. I could not feel the bottom of the bath with my hands and I clawed at the water, fighting my way to the surface. I couldn't keep my mouth shut much longer, but just as I opened it, I reached the surface of her bath, my mouth filling with fragrant air. I grabbed the side of the bathtub and held on. Relieved, I breathed deeply, drawing in María's smells.

Calming myself, I remembered Señor Prado and his own near drowning in the river. I couldn't help feeling proud. We shared something.

———————

That night my mother returned from Rosa's village. She built a fire with small sticks on the floor in the kitchen. She spent several minutes stoking the fire and then placed a kettle on a brick in the center. In a minute the water boiled and she poured me a cup of coffee.

I asked about Rosa, and my mother told me Rosa was fine, although her labor had been difficult. It had dragged over two days, but the baby, a baby girl, was healthy and large, enormous even.

The fire was fading now, already fading. The sticks burned nearly as fast as paper. "Mother," I said, and I felt silly asking what I was about to ask, "Mother, have you ever seen María?"

My mother didn't laugh, as I expected her to. I could hardly see her face; the fire was now no more than a few orange embers.

"María's a very beautiful girl," she said. "She was an *indígena* queen not long ago."

"But have you seen her?"

"I'm sure she's just shy with young boys. She's a modest girl, despite everything. Why do you need to look at her, anyway? Just do your work and you'll be fine."

The room was now completely dark. The night seemed to have swallowed us.

"But Mother . . ." I protested.

"Shh," she said. "Just do your work. We need the money. Please remember. I'm tired now. I had a long walk. Don't talk to me. You can come to my bed and sing. Will you do that?"

I stood beside her bed in the darkness and sang a song about a long trip a queen makes to find her daughter.

Despite my mother's admonition, I was determined to see María. Fixed on my obsession, I couldn't sleep. I left my house before even the most bravo rooster had split the air with his call and arrived at María's house an hour earlier than usual. After removing my shoes at the door to the toolroom, I sneaked into the kitchen. I heard a sound coming from the dining room, a soft sound, someone chewing. I thought: María's eating breakfast.

I knew I had to be careful about my next step. I crouched beside the entrance to the dining room. The sound had stopped. Had I been discovered? I caught my breath.

The sound began again, a delightful munching. She was giggling as she ate. Silently, I lay flat on the floor. I slid on my stomach to where I could place my head in the entrance to the dining room. I looked up but could see nothing, not even her feet below the table. I lifted myself with my arms. Still nothing. Finally I risked everything—my job, my life—and stood.

Something black and white with a long face—a skunk or *pizote*—jumped from the table and raced past me. I held a scream in my throat. I held it for a minute, two perhaps. Finally I swallowed it and let it sink to my belly.

My hands were trembling. I breathed deeply several times, trying to calm myself, but my breath raced out of me. I slumped against the wall and slid to the floor. I felt as if the blood had been drained from me. I wanted to cry.

After a few minutes my trembling subsided. I stood up. I cleared the plate and glass from the table, washed them and returned them to the cupboard. I listened and heard nothing. I looked around, wondering if the animal were staring at me from some corner or crevice or cupboard. I wondered if María were looking at me from somewhere, some hole in the wall, some crack in the ceiling.

I had more than an hour before I needed to begin my work. My curiosity returned, and with it my courage. Softly, slowly, I walked into Señor Prado's study and toward the shelf with the white books. I was interested in what Señor Prado called his memoirs. I wanted to know what he did after the woman in the river disappeared.

I looked around for animals, for eyes. Nothing. I picked the first white book from the shelf and opened it. The pages were blank. There were at least two hundred pages in the book and none of them had words. I returned the book to the shelf and pulled the second book off. This book, too, was empty. I looked at the third book, the fourth, the fifth. Empty. I opened each of the twenty-four books on the shelf and discovered the same blankness.

I heard a noise like a laugh. I looked around, my heart drilling a hole in my chest. Silence again. I returned the last book to the shelf and crept out of Señor Prado's study. I began to sweep the kitchen, my body shaking as if I'd discovered a dead man.

In the closet, I listened. Again, I pressed my ear against the door, hoping to hear María enter, to feel the vibrations of her feet on the tile. Nothing.

"*Okinik.*"

I opened the door and sat down, surrounded by her smell.

"Do you have a gun?" María asked. "If you have a gun, it will be easier to kill him."

"Kill who?"

"Señor Prado."

"Why would I kill him?"

She sighed. "Don't you love me yet?"

I had learned not to delay. "Yes."

"Good." She laughed gently. "Good. Do you have a gun?"

"No."

"Not good. No, this is a problem."

"I can get a gun. My brother, Augusto, always carries a gun. He takes it to the cantinas."

"You can borrow it?"

"Yes. I'll take it when he's sleeping. He sleeps like he's dead. I'll take it when he comes home again."

"When will that be?"

"I don't know."

"We don't have much time. Each moment he's alive is a miracle."

"I could borrow your gun," I said.

She laughed mockingly. "How will I defend myself when they come after me?"

"Who will come after you?"

"The people that kill him will want to kill me, too. They'll consider me a witness and they won't want me around."

"We could kill him first. There wouldn't be other people to worry about. You could be hiding already. You could be in the mountains with my mother."

"You have a nice plan for someone who doesn't even want to kill Señor Prado. You don't want to kill him, do you?"

"No. But I love you."

"That's something. That's a start. But you don't hate Señor Prado?"

"No."

"Then you won't kill him. You'll take my gun and you might even want to kill him to please me, but you won't. And he'll take the gun from you and then neither of us will have a gun. But if you hated him, hated him like I do, you could kill him. We don't have much time. And there's not much I can do. But I can try." She paused. "I hate Señor Prado."

Her remark filled the silence, echoed faintly off the walls.

"I hated him when he first came to my father's house. He had three bodyguards then. They formed a triangle around him. They were little men, and Señor Prado stood in the middle of them like a giant. He was as tall as our ceiling.

"My father was short, shorter than the bodyguards. He spoke hardly any Spanish. He worked at a coffee plantation. He was the second in charge, the assistant manager. He did everything Don Rafael, the manager, a man like Señor Prado, asked him to do. My father was impressed with big men who spoke only Spanish.

"My father didn't know how rich Señor Prado was. It wouldn't have mattered anyway. My father's imagination could only stretch so far. And Señor Prado's riches were more than any *campesino* could dream of.

"Señor Prado told my father that he wanted to make an arrangement with him. He said he wanted me to work for him. That's the way he put it. 'Don Palush,' he said to my father, 'I would like your daughter to work for me.'

"My father, of course, was flattered to be called 'don' by such an important man. He said, 'Yes, of course, she needs work. All people must work.'

"Señor Prado said, 'This is special work in a house I own. And she will do it for the rest of her life. It's good work and I'll treat her well. She'll live in the house and she'll only have to work certain days.'

"My father didn't understand. I think the Spanish words were too complicated. He nodded and said, 'All people must work.'

"Señor Prado said, 'I'll pay a great price for the work your daughter does. I'll pay her with the beautiful house she'll live in and the fine food she'll eat. And I'll pay you in cash.'

"My father understood the last word. He nodded and said, 'All people must work. Yes, work is good. How much?'

"My father was not stupid. He was poor, but he was not stupid. 'How much?' he asked.

"Señor Prado told my father to name his price. I watched my father's face. He was thinking hard. He was thinking how much he could ask for his daughter. But I knew my imagination was greater than my father's. I knew I could think of a bigger number. I spoke from the dark corner of the room. I said, 'Fifty thousand.'

"'Quetzales,' Señor Prado said, looking at my father. 'Fifty thousand quetzales.' My father smiled. This was a lot of money, more than he could make in a lifetime.

"'Dollars,' I said. 'United States dollars.'

"Señor Prado smiled. 'She's smart,' he said. 'Beautiful and smart. She knows about dollars. How does she know I have dollars?'

"He looked at me now, for the first time. Looked straight through those heavy glasses and into my eyes. I think this was the only time he ever saw me. He knew right then. He knew we would have a war. But he knew he had all the soldiers and all the guns. He thought the war would be quick.

"'Fifty thousand dollars,' I said.

"Señor Prado smiled again. 'Fifty thousand dollars,' he said. 'Is this agreeable to you, Don Palush?'

"My father nodded. He didn't know what he was hearing. He knew 'fifty thousand.' But he didn't know what a dollar was. He didn't know it was five times more valuable than our currency.

"Señor Prado didn't give my father fifty thousand dollars. He gave him a coffee plantation worth that much and more. My father, a poor man who had never made more than enough to keep us fed with beans and tortillas all year, was now a *finquiero*.

"I know Señor Prado expected my father to fail. Let a clown be king. Yes, I'm sure Señor Prado expected my father to fail. But the first year my father owned the coffee plantation, he made more money from it than Señor Prado ever had. The price of coffee was very high and the workers worked hard for my father, I don't know why. They didn't respect him. He was just a *campesino* like they were.

"So my father was a success. But he was old, and the next year, even as the coffee beans grew as big as cherries, he died.

"My brothers inherited the land, but they were not good managers like my father, and besides, the land was not as valuable in little blocks. One by one, my brothers sold the land back to Señor Prado. He didn't pay dollars for any of it.

"So that is the story. Do you see why I hate Señor Prado?"

"Yes," I said.

"But I haven't hated him every minute. He didn't touch me for months after he put me in this house. He was as gentle as a bird, singing to me from a distance. I wondered why he had bought me if he didn't want me. When he finally did have me, I wanted him too."

She sighed.

"After a while, of course, he relaxed. He thought he had me won, even if I hadn't given him a baby. He thought he had my heart. And so he was himself. He let me see him. Men declare victory too early. They celebrate with their enemies. I'm alive. And he's about to die."

───────────

Walking up the mountain, I imagined María as my wife come to live with me in my village. And at night, in my bed, I imagined her beside me, warm and fragrant, with her hair falling all around her. I was almost seventeen, and several boys in the village my age had already married, their wives nursing babies while grinding corn in *molinos*.

But I couldn't see María wanting to live in a tiny house in my village. I thought if I could return to school, could become a doctor or a lawyer, I could buy María a big house, a castle. She could tend bees in a large field behind the house. To become a doctor or lawyer, however, I would have had to study for six or seven more years, and I doubted María would have wanted to wait.

Ignoring my doubts, I conjured a María soft and warm beside me in bed. Even this part of my dream I couldn't sustain: I would be too thin and little for her, hardly enough for her to hold. She was too large for my bed, too large for my house and village. Too large for me ever to have. Or too small, perhaps. Invisible. She was only a voice, a song from ancient days, telling me about all we'd lost and all we had yet to lose. But—no—if I could hold her, perhaps I would lose nothing. Perhaps I would gain the world.

The radishes were almost ready, the tiny red heads emerging from the soil. Sitting on the bathroom floor, I told María this. "You've done well," she said. "You made up for your mistake. Soon we'll be feasting on radishes. All because of you. You deserve some reward." Then she astonished me: "Would you like to bathe with me?"

Her voice contained her familiar, mocking laughter, but I ignored it and chased my desire: "Yes."

"Well, all right. But do you see that blue towel on the rack in front of you? Yes? Good. First take off your shirt. All right. Now wrap that towel around your head. Wrap it so that it covers your eyes. Have you done that? You know that if you don't, I'll shoot you. This is the rule. If the towel falls off, you die, understand? Good. You are my *metz*, but you must learn to love me for who I am, not what you think I am."

I tied the towel around my eyes so tight that I thought I might have cut off the blood to my head. I felt light-headed, drunk, too happy to be alive.

"Now take off your pants," María said.

"What?"

"Take off your pants. You can't bathe with your pants on."

I took off my pants and felt small and cold.

"Now your underpants."

I hesitated. But I was reminded of Señor Prado's hesitation with the woman in the river, and I took off my underpants. "Good," she said. "Now step into the bath on the far end. Take a few steps to your right. One more. Good. Now come in."

With my hand, I felt the edge of the bath. I stepped over it. The water was scalding. I gritted my teeth. María laughed.

"Too hot?" she asked. "You can leave if you'd like."

"No," I said, and put my other foot in. I felt as if I were going to melt, and I had to resist the urge to scream. I crouched, and the water burned my buttocks, but I was silent, despite the intense pain. Biting my lip, I lowered my waist into the water and my buttocks touched bottom. I was in María's bath. The pain passed. My body no longer throbbed but felt soothed.

"Do you feel it?" she asked.

"Feel what?"

"My toe."

I concentrated but couldn't feel anything. "No."

"The big toe of your right foot is touching the big toe of my left foot."

I tried to feel it, but it was difficult to sense any single part of my body. Touched everywhere by an enveloping, luxurious warmth, I could only imagine what her toe must feel like, a light pressure, a tickle.

"Yes, I feel it," I said.

"Do you want to feel all of me?" she asked.

"Yes."

"Then you have to swim toward me on your back."

"What?"

"Paddle with your arms and kick with your legs. I'll count to five, in Pokomchí." She laughed. "On five, start swimming. *Jenaj, quib, xib, quejeb, ho'ob!*"

I thrashed madly with my arms and legs. Scalding water shot into my mouth and choked me. I slid under, still kicking, and swallowed burning water. I reached for the bottom of the bathtub to lift myself, but I couldn't find it. When I reached for the sides, I couldn't feel them either. I swallowed more water and began to cough. I thought I would die. I coughed, swallowed, coughed, and felt a blackness invade my eyes.

Then I was kneeling in the bathtub and breathing cool air. I opened my eyes. I no longer had on the blindfold. I could see the bath. María was gone.

When I finished singing for my mother, I said, "Mother, do you think María's crazy?"

The wind was fierce, and I heard it rush through the cornstalks in the nearby fields. I heard it slice through the cracks in our abode house. It chilled me.

"What are you saying?" my mother said.

"Is María crazy?"

"Why do you speak like this?"

"She tells me strange things. She tells me that Señor Prado is going to die soon. She tells me all the evil things he's done."

"María is a lonely girl. Her loneliness makes her sad."

"Is she lying, Mother?"

"I don't know. We shouldn't become involved with these people. They have their lives and we have ours. We can work for them. That's fine. We need money. But the less we say to them and them to us, the better. We have our own ways."

"But María had no choice."

"Her father was a poor man. Señor Prado gave him a lot of money. All poor men are fools in front of money."

"Is María crazy, Mother?"

"She's lonely, child. She's lonely. Don't speak to her. She'll say anything not to be lonely. And don't speak to Señor Prado. Do your work and come home. You can speak to me."

"Have you ever seen María, Mother?"

"She's a beautiful girl. But she's lonely."

"But have you seen her?"

"I'm sleeping, child. I'm sleeping."

"I love her. I love her, Mother."

But my mother was asleep.

I saw Señor Prado's helicopter from the window of the library. It was as if its blades were chopping up the sky. I ran downstairs and put the pots of water on the stove. Then I retreated to the toolroom. I didn't want to see Señor Prado, not after what María had told me and what I'd done with her. At the same time I wanted to hear the end of his story, even if he was making it up, pretending, for whatever reason, to be reading his memoirs. I believed there was something in his story for me, something, I hoped, beautiful.

One of Señor Prado's bodyguards entered the toolroom and said, "Señor Prado would like you to listen to him again. Sit at the foot of his chair and don't move."

I stepped gingerly into Señor Prado's study. "Well," he said, "are you ready for the conclusion?"

"Yes, señor!"

"Good, good. Sit down." He stared at the white book he held in his hand, and when I sat down, he opened it and began to speak: "I had come so close the last time, had been in the same water with her. Had I had more courage, or had I been a better swimmer, I would have had her.

"I stayed out every night and prowled the desert like a hungry dog. I didn't merely inhabit the desert, I was the desert. I was all its heat, I was all its thirst. For weeks I did this, and the longer I did, the more desperate I became to see her.

"One night, exhausted, I fell on the desert sand, and I knew I was going to die. I was starving and tired and thirsty. I had given up. I was ready for God to take me. But then her voice came to me, soft and low, like a cat's purr. I forced myself to stand and look around. When standing, however, I couldn't hear her. I dropped on the sand, and I heard her voice again. I listened to the sand. I followed her voice, crawling.

"Her voice led me to the shore of the river, but so far away from town that I couldn't see any lights; behind me was only darkness, a night so black I wondered if I'd died. I couldn't see anything in the blackness. No moon lit up the river. I looked hard, my eyes heavy with exhaustion. Then I saw her, as if she'd emerged out of the air above the water. She was faint, fainter than a dying match in a forest. I crawled to the bank of the river. She glowed stronger now, the light heating up within her.

"I stood, kicked off my sandals, and placed my toes in the water. The cold water stung like a scorpion. Determined, I walked in. The light grew even stronger within her, so strong it shed a small path on the water, the path I walked. The water was up to my knees, then my chest. I knew I would have to swim to where she stood, safe on some sandbar.

"Although the current was strong, I didn't hesitate. I fell forward and began to slash through it. The current shoved me downstream. I fought back, pounding it angrily, as if it were trying to strangle me.

"When I could pound no longer, when I felt the water was going to carry me away, my feet touched bottom, the sandbar, and I was standing close enough to see the freckle on her upper lip. It was her only imperfection, but it was what she needed to make her truly beautiful. She glowed now like a fire. I was close enough to touch her, and I lifted my hands to feel her. She opened her mouth, and I knew she was about to speak. I shouldn't have stopped. Had I ignored her, she would have been mine. I could have pulled her to me in the rushing river, could have wrapped my arms around her glowing body. Instead, I hesitated, listening, curious and frightened.

"She said: 'You must find me forever.'

"Then I was staring at the sun, a great, blinding spot of yellow and orange. I cried out and fell backward into the rushing water. I was taken away, taken under, and I swallowed the stinging cold water and it filled my stomach like poison. I was ready to die, asking for it, but I felt hands on my shoulders and I was lifted out of the water into light and air.

"A young cowboy with a mustache held me up like a baby. 'Well, boy,' he said, 'you just about drowned.' He carried me to shore, sat me on a rock, and pounded my back until all the water had spilled out of my stomach. The water had been so cold coming in, but now it was hotter than coffee; it was like I was spitting out liquid fire.

"I was too tired and dazed to move. I watched the cowboy wash his T-shirt and socks. After he'd finished, he sat on a rock next to me and asked me if I was hungry. I was starving, but when he scrambled some eggs over a fire, I could eat only two bites before my stomach revolted. I told him thank you and then walked away.

"I looked for her every night for a week, tramping through the desert, but I knew it was hopeless. I cursed her aloud and in my thoughts and in my dreams. I felt wasted, my insides torn up as if she had slipped a machete inside me and jiggled it for a year.

"I heard her words every hour, a soft torment, a tease. 'You must find me forever.' Finally I decided that if she expected me to look for her, she could go to the devil. She could walk into my bedroom as naked as the moon and I would turn over and keep sleeping.

"But of course she didn't come. She was gone, and she knew I would never forget her. 'You must find me forever.'

"And now, of course, I know she was right. 'You must find me forever.' I've made myself the richest man in the country. I've torn down buildings and put up buildings. I've killed men and had men kill each other. I'm looking for her. 'You must find me forever.' That's what I've done."

He closed the book. He smiled, a big, toothy grin. "Well?" he asked.

I opened my mouth, but I couldn't think of anything to say. It was not the beautiful ending I'd hoped for, and I was afraid—of what awaited me now, tomorrow, as long as I lived.

"I'm an old man," he said. "I'm a few steps from peace and I'm walking very fast." He smiled reassuringly.

"Here," he said, holding out the book. "Return this to the shelf."

I stood and stepped up to him slowly. He did not have his gun ready, and I was glad. Cautiously, I reached for the book. I held it, but his hands resisted, and I was nervous, wondering if this were a trick. My grip tightened and his eased, but as I pulled the book free, he grabbed me by the throat. He jerked me to his chest and wrapped his enormous forearm around my neck.

"Don't you think I know when my books have been touched?" he hissed. "I can smell your fingerprints, boy. So you know the truth. I'm illiterate. I never learned to read and write. I clawed my way up from the desert. I can't write my history, but I have it; just as sure as I could kill you with the slightest jerk of my arm, I have it."

He tightened his grip briefly, a jolt that shocked my heart.

"I'm blind, but I can smell like a dog looking for a bitch. And before I kill you, I want you to remember something. I want you to take this to heaven with you. I can't write, but I have a history. My people have a history. We can't always write it, but we're making it. You can see our history in the buildings we've built, in the roads we've carved up through the mountains. You can see it in the sons and daughters we've fathered all over this country.

"You think you have a history, you stupid Indians. You think that because your history is ancient, it's immortal. But history is only as lasting as the people who remember it. And we're eliminating your history year by year. We marry your sisters and pull their *cortes* off them and get them to speak our language. The army fills its ranks with Indian soldiers and sends them off to kill Indian guerrillas. Better than putting them all in concentration camps. Oh, of course the army bombs your villages too. Can't be too subtle. But it all adds up to the same thing, doesn't it? Little by little, you'll forget who you are and your sisters will forget who they are. And their children will never know. They'll end up thinking they're like us. But why not? Their blood will be our blood.

"But María, terrible, beautiful María, won't have my child. I tried, believe me I tried. Those first few years, I was as hungry as a horse. I tried. I don't understand. She wasn't taking anything, she wasn't putting anything between her legs to stop my soldiers from marching inside her. I told her she was infertile, but she just giggled at me like I was a clown.

"She wants to kill me, like everyone else. She wants to kill me, and she could do it anytime. She could do it when we're in the bathtub. She has a pistol. I bought it for her! She could put a bullet in my brain any time. I wouldn't be able to see it coming.

"But she'd be caught. And she's not willing to make that exchange, her life for mine. Isn't that funny? A little *indígena* girl in exchange for a millionaire. Does she think she's worth a million? Does she think her life is equal to mine? Yes, she does.

Amazing, she does. Why? Because she can bring little *indígena* babies into the world."

Señor Prado laughed, but his laughter stopped quickly. "Why? So they can populate the mountains in poverty? So they can go beg on the streets of big cities and die like rats? She thinks they can reclaim this country. She thinks there will be Indian kings again. She dreams bigger dreams than I do, but she's just a servant and I'm a king. I'm a king."

It surprised me, what followed. Señor Prado started to cry, tears that shook his body.

"She's waiting for one of the others to come and kill me. And they will; one of these days, they will. I'm strong even if I'm blind, but I can't beat them all. One of them will find a way to kill me. But María won't survive. She'd be better off killing me now and going to jail and having a baby with an *indígena* prison guard. I bought her; she's mine. There are instructions. When I die, she dies too."

He pulled his forearm hard around me, but I also felt his other arm wrap around my waist and pull me close, lightly, as if he were hugging me. I felt his tears on my forehead even as I felt my breath leave me. I saw the light fade and the darkness come.

I heard myself gasp. My breathing sounded off the walls of María's bathroom. I was in her empty bathtub, the curtain drawn.

"You don't have much time," María said, from behind the curtain. "You've got to kill him now. He's leaving."

She paused, and I heard the helicopter's blades slicing the air.

"I saved you, now you save me," she said. "I'll leave my pistol on the floor. Before he steps on his helicopter, shoot him. Both bodyguards will be on the helicopter, helping him up. If you shoot him, they won't get down. They'll leave. They're cowards. Why shouldn't they be? Señor Prado isn't their brother.

"Shoot him, do you understand? Kill him and then come for me. All right? Kill him and we'll leave together. I'm putting my pistol on the floor."

Although I was aching and groggy, I understood. She wanted me to kill Señor Prado. And I was ready. I loved her. But did I hate Señor Prado?

I had trouble standing. I felt as if I were carrying a man on my shoulders. My blood pounded against my forehead and beat against my eyes. For a few seconds, I saw only a dizzy red pattern.

After pushing the curtain aside, I picked María's pistol off the floor. It was silver and cold. I walked to the door. It was locked. María was hiding in the bathroom closet. I could have opened it and seen her, and this occurred to me briefly, but only briefly. I unlocked the door and walked out.

The helicopter was in the front yard, its blades beating the air. I opened the front door and saw the two bodyguards jump on board. I lifted my pistol and aimed it at Señor Prado's back. He had a few steps left before he reached the helicopter.

My right hand, the hand that held the pistol, was shaking. I placed my left hand against the cold shaft to steady it. I watched him walk. Shoot him, I told myself. Shoot him now. I followed him, staring just above the barrel of the pistol. His bodyguards were reaching for him, offering him their hands as he placed his right foot on the single metal step. Shoot him now, I said. Shoot him now.

I breathed deeply, my last breath before I became a murderer.

The gunfire filled the air before I'd completed my breath, and I dove to the ground. I couldn't tell where the shots were coming from, but I saw Señor Prado's body leak blood. He fell forward, his head smashing against the helicopter stair. The helicopter lifted off, and his bodyguards retreated into its dark interior. The helicopter fled into the sky.

I jumped up, turned, and ran, my blood crashing against my skull. I ran through the hall and living room and out the tool-room into the backyard. I raced across the radish garden. I raced with the speed of a hundred rabbits into the forest, and I ran until I couldn't feel my legs under me. I wondered if I were flying.

Finally, I fell, caught by some vine or fallen branch. I fell, and my head slammed into the dirt. Darkness invaded me.

When I woke up, I heard crickets singing. I heard dogs barking deep in the night. I heard, from another land, it seemed, the faint hum of automobiles.

I stood. My head throbbed, and when I touched it, I felt dried blood. The night was cold and a slight rain was falling. The tiny drops, as fine as needle points, pricked my skin and helped me conquer the dullness in my brain.

I walked back through the damp forest toward the house.

The house was vast, lonely, and barely visible in the darkness. I was sure María had escaped. Señor Prado was dead; the bodyguards were gone. María must have escaped. No one was left. No one was left anywhere, it seemed. The emptiness was complete. Or was María waiting?

I had to be certain. I crept toward the house and reached the backdoor, the door to the toolroom. It was open, as I had left it. I slipped inside.

I knew María's house as well as I knew my own. I knew I would have no trouble negotiating my way in the dark. But first I needed to be certain I was alone.

I stood in the middle of the toolroom and listened. From the kitchen, I heard a faint hissing sound, like a chorus of snakes. I shuddered. But the hissing was steady, too steady to be coming from a person or animal, and I calmed myself. I crept into the living room, stepping lightly. Peering around the edge of the kitchen door, I saw the two stoves, their burners spitting out fire. I stepped into the kitchen and snapped off the burners, terminating their fruitless heating of empty pots.

I listened again. Silence.

I entered the living room and began to walk across it, but my knee touched something soft. I jumped back, bumping the coffee table, which screeched against the tile floor. My heart pounded against my chest.

The jaguar was in the center of the living room. I maneuvered past it, careful, my steps as small and as quiet as a bird's. I reached the end of the living room, and on the floor of the hallway I saw a faint dab of light. I clung to the walls, staying in the shadows. I circled the spot carefully. I circled it until my back was pressed against the front door. The light was coming from the top of the stairs, from the bathroom.

I walked up the stairs, my heart chattering against my chest. I walked quickly, needing my momentum. I reached the bathroom. The door had been broken down and lay in splinters on the bathroom floor.

I walked toward the curtain and was ready to pull it aside when I heard María's voice: "You've come."

I stopped, steadying myself by putting my hand against the wall.

"I'm glad you've come," she said.

"Let's go," I said, breathing hard. "Let's go to my village. Let's go now."

She giggled, her delightful giggle.

"Why in such a hurry?"

"They could come back."

"Who?"

"The people who killed Señor Prado."

"Oh, so you didn't kill Señor Prado?"

"No. I . . ." I paused. I remembered holding the gun, waiting until my nerve caught up with my intention. "No, I had the gun pointed at him, but someone else fired first."

"I see."

"There were a lot of bullets. I thought they might have been trying to kill me. I . . ." I paused again. I bowed my head. "I ran."

Guilty, I waited for her response.

"María?"

Silence.

"Let's go, María. Let's go."

"María?"

Silence.

I took a step closer to the bathtub and gripped the curtain.

"María?"

"María? Let's go, María!"

"María?"

I pulled the curtain aside.

The bathtub was filled with blood. As I gazed at it, it seemed to stretch as long as a river and to run, fierce in its flow, from one end of our country to the other. Somewhere in all the blood was María. If I saw her it was only as I'd always seen her—mother, sister, lover—and she was beautiful.

Gemelas

When pushed open, the twin doors of the bakery made a distinctive sound. The sound was not like the long growl of the *pulman* bus climbing the hill toward town nor the hacking cough of the local bus rumbling down the hill toward Cobán. It was softer than these sounds, yet louder than a boot stepping across gravel or chalk marking up a blackboard.

The sound was not pleasant, just as the sounds of the buses could not be called pleasant. But it wasn't an unpleasant sound either. It was merely a familiar sound, a sound Rocío heard every morning after she opened the rusting lock with the bent key, a sound almost, but not quite, like stiff wind rushing across sand.

How many people knew this sound, she wondered, knew it well

enough to anticipate it, to imitate it with a low whistle? Only her twin sister, Anabella. Anabella worked in the bakery in the afternoon, and after lunch she, too, had to open the bakery doors. The background sounds, Rocío thought, would be different for Anabella. The *pulman* wouldn't be climbing toward town; instead, several trucks, whose motors made sounds like corn being ground, would be idling on the street in front of the bakery. And there would be the sounds of a hundred footsteps as people walked to and from the market across the street. Yet Anabella would hear this sound, this light scrape of the doors on the cement floor of the bakery, and knowing this, Rocío felt proud and defeated.

There was, now more than ever, something glorious about being like her sister. Anabella, as everyone said, was beautiful, with skin as pale as morning and hair thick and black and falling past her waist. Rocío had the same face, of course, the same hair, and she knew that those who praised her sister would, of necessity, have to praise her also, although lately her own beauty was seldom described in the way her sister's was; her pale skin, for instance, was seen as a sign of an impending fever. And people who knew the twins well had always made deeper distinctions. When they were little, their grandmother told them that Anabella looked like their father and Rocío like their mother. But their grandmother was half-blind then—this was just a year or two before she died—so what did she know?

In a month Anabella would marry Roger Buenafe, who owned a coffee plantation just outside of Santa Cruz, a plantation that encompassed an entire village and encroached on three more. Every girl wanted to be Anabella López, beautiful and, very soon, very rich, and Rocío López was about as close to being Anabella as a girl could get without actually being her. She was, of course, regularly mistaken for Anabella, and walking through the market on the day Anabella announced her wedding, she heard the *indígena* women, hovering over their tomatoes and tortillas, whisper Anabella's name, and she lifted her chin higher, high enough to feel on her eyes the pleasant sting of sunlight that sneaked through the cracks in the ceiling.

And yet there was something frustrating and annoying in the fact that there were so few things uniquely hers, that even something as insignificant as the sound the bakery doors made on being opened was not hers alone, that this, too, she shared with Anabella. Every day, she experienced déjà vu, not the ethereal sensation of having, in some past life, taken the same steps, seen the same things, but the knowledge that her sister had taken those steps and done those things, and perhaps—no, almost certainly—thought the same thoughts; or if she hadn't, she would. Because Santa Cruz was such a tiny town, it was hard to experience anything unique, and almost impossible if you were a twin.

Rocío found consolation in her sister's impending marriage. From her wedding day on, Anabella's life would revolve around the distinction of her being Anabella López de Buenafe. The rhythm and texture of her life would be different from Rocío's; instead of the scrape of doors and the warm smell of bread, Anabella would, Rocío imagined, soon hear the rustle of workers in the field as they picked coffee beans and, before long, smell a baby's new breath.

Rocío knew that had her mother assigned her the afternoon shift at the family bakery instead of Anabella, she would be the one getting married, she would be the one every girl in town would be speaking of with envy and admiration. It was at the bakery that Roger Buenafe met Anabella. He stopped in to buy bread one afternoon after dropping off a truckload of coffee at the distributor's in Cobán, and he struck up a conversation with Anabella, which was, as Anabella later reported, light and harmless. But it was enough to bring him back the next afternoon, and the next, until, despite the full bags of bread he carried away with him after each visit, everyone in town knew he was more interested in Anabella than sweet bread.

Rocío's friends, who were also Anabella's friends, wondered if Rocío was jealous of Anabella, and Rocío told them no, although this was not true. She *was* jealous of Anabella, jealous that Anabella had been touched by the hand of fate and a coffee prince. But her jealousy was not strong, not overwhelming. She did not remain awake nights, turning over in the bed she and Anabella shared, condemning her mother for giving her the morning shift at the bakery. She was happy for Anabella because she loved her sister and genuinely wanted her sister to be happy, and she was happy, too, because from the day of Anabella's wedding, there would, at last, be a distinct path for each of them to travel.

On their first day of elementary school, their teacher had looked at them, clapped her hands, and said with delight, "Oh, look, *gemelas*." Twins. And *gemelas* is how Rocío and Anabella became known, both collectively and, with the *s* dropped, individually. It was custom to identify someone by his or her appearance. In that first-grade class alone there were a Chinito, because he looked Chinese, a Gordita, because she was fat, and a Payaso Pelón, because he had a broad and befuddled face and wore a perpetual crew cut on account of persistent lice. The nicknames stayed the same, even when the people who bore them didn't. Gordita remained Gordita even after fifth grade, when, because of illness, she became as thin as a cornstalk.

Rocío was known as *gemela* to even her closest friends, girls who stopped by her house in the late afternoon on their sweep of the streets and sang along with the radio on Rocío and Anabella's dresser before staring at their plastic watches and gasping at the time, saying their fathers would punish them for being out so late. Sometimes Rocío and Anabella would go with these girls on their visits, and they would stop at Gordita's house or Hidalia's house and sing with the radio there or laugh about the way Pulga had danced atop his desk when he mistakenly thought Don Carlos, the teacher, was out of the room.

These excursions were fun, but more often the twins elected to stay home in their room, giggling at nothing. When their friends left, they were glad, and they would sit cross-legged on their bed and stare into each other's eyes until one of them smiled, and more often than not they smiled at the same time. Or they would take turns combing each other's hair in front of the two-meter-tall mirror that their father, in one of his rare trips to the capital, had found discarded beside a movie theater.

If there was something humiliatingly impersonal in being known as *gemela*, then the indignity was balanced by the fact that there was, thankfully, someone with whom to share the moniker. On nights when they could not sleep, they would kick each other beneath the sheets, at first unintentionally, then with more purposeful vigor. Rocío or Anabella would call the other *gemela*, as someone might utter a bad word. The only way to achieve a more potent insult was to say the word louder, and so they would call each other *gemela* with increasing volume until the episode ended, as always, with a "shh" from their mother, sewing in the next room, and their triumphant giggles.

They attended school together until the day Roger Buenafe proposed to Anabella and, her future secure, Anabella quit. There had, however, been a time when, because of school, Rocío thought she would shake Anabella, would bolt ahead of her down life's trail. It was after the mathematics final in ninth grade, a test neither had studied for. Rocío thought, with her customary confidence, that she had done fine, at least a ninety. Anabella, on the other hand, was certain she had flunked and flunked badly enough to have flunked the class. That night, talking in their bed as moonlight fell through the tiny holes in their tin roof like sand falling through a sifter, Anabella said, "It looks like you'll be going to *colegio* alone."

Rocío imagined Anabella's words as prophecy and saw herself taking the bus in the afternoon to Cobán, where she would attend *colegio*—Santa Cruz was too small a town to have its own secondary school—while her sister, sadly, remained in Santa Cruz, retaking math at the junior high. In her vision, Rocío didn't get past the bus ride; there was so much to discover even there. What would it be like, this bus ride, this journey alone, the window open and her hair blowing back, her hair long enough to patter against the nose of the person behind her? There would, perhaps, be someone she didn't know on the bus, some boy from San Cristóbal, the town to the west, who would be on his way to the same *colegio* and would fall in love with her right there. Perhaps it would be his nose that her hair would be pattering.

But there was, too, something unsettling about the possibility of studying in Cobán without her sister. Rocío's mind turned from the bus ride to the troubling thought of having to navigate a world without Anabella, of having to bear the world's full force instead of halving its blow with her sister. That night, she dreamed she saw the earth split open on the street in front of the town square, and the giant crack filled with water, a canal. Anabella was on one side and Rocío on the other. All Rocío could think to tell her sister was "Jump," although neither of them could swim.

As it turned out, Anabella had been needlessly worried. She scored an eighty-four on her math exam, two points better than Rocío.

They both had boyfriends in the tenth grade, when they did, in fact, take the bus together in the afternoons to Cobán to study at Colegio Verapaz. It was the first time that either of them had had a serious relationship with a boy. For Rocío, it was at first a magical experience. She enjoyed the sensation of having been someplace where no one had been before when, crossing the *colegio's* basketball court, sliding down the bank and camping beneath the skinny pine trees, she kissed Edvin full on the mouth and tasted his tongue on her teeth. Anabella and Hugo preferred an even more remote spot, behind the experimental cornfields of the neighboring agricultural college.

Rocío and Anabella were uncommunicative about their relationships, shunning conversation in bed in order to close their eyes, feel the cool night play against parts of their bodies sticking out from the sheets, and dream of their boyfriends.

After two months, Edvin begged Rocío to make love to him, begged with a squint in his eyes, as if fighting the sun (even though they were in the shade of a thin pine), and a plea in his voice, as if he had his hand in a pot of boiling water and wanted her to remove it. She rebuffed his advance, and she thought she had defeated his desire forever. A week later, however, the squint and plea returned. Again she rebuffed him, annoyed that her refusal had stood only seven days before the next assault but fascinated by his desire and flattered that she was its object. With pride, she broke the nighttime silence with Anabella: "Edvin wants to sleep with me." Anabella rolled over, looked at her sister, and said, "Hugo wants to sleep with me." A silence followed, as if they were mourning something, but then they laughed, laughed until their mother whispered "shh" from the next room. "*Gemela*," Anabella said and kissed her sister on the lips. "*Gemela*," Rocío said and returned the kiss. They laughed again before falling asleep.

The next day they said good-bye to their boyfriends.

It wasn't until after their eleventh-grade year that Rocío and

Anabella were put to work in their father's bakery. They had visited the bakery on many occasions, watching their mother or, when their mother became older, the women their father hired, sell bread—the sugary *pan dulce* and the half-sweet and tender *ricado* and the plain but popular *pan francés*—which their father made in a building behind the bakery's storefront. At age eighteen they were, their mother decided, old enough to contribute to the family's income, and during their long vacation after the school year ended in October, Rocío was assigned the morning shift and Anabella the afternoon shift.

When Rocío rose at seven in the morning, time enough to eat breakfast and be at the bakery by eight, Anabella also rose. They had always risen together. They had always needed to rise together. Anabella even walked up the street with Rocío toward the bakery, and they nodded as people greeted them with waves and shouts of "*Buenos días, gemelas.*"

Before unlocking the doors, Rocío turned to her sister. Anabella was in the full morning sunlight, looking paler than a white nun orchid. Rocío wanted to propose that they work both shifts together, but instead she said, "I'll walk you here in the afternoon." Anabella smiled and turned away.

Anabella no longer needed to get up with Rocío in the mornings. She always awoke with Rocío but stayed in bed. When Rocío dressed, Anabella would wrap herself in the sheets like a bird building a nest around itself.

Rocío had little to do in preparation for Anabella's wedding. Roger Buenafe was paying for everything, even Anabella's dress, which a tailor in Cobán was making from a picture Roger had seen in an American magazine, one of those movie-star wedding dresses with the train as long as the church aisle. Roger himself was having a tuxedo made by the same tailor, with tails flying out the back like crow's wings. The wedding would not be held in the Santa Cruz Catholic Church, an aging edifice that only recently had been repaired after the earthquake fifteen years earlier had shot a crack down the middle. For a man of Roger's stature, only the church in Cobán, which seated a hundred more people than the church in Santa Cruz, would do. He had hired three buses to take people the fifteen kilometers from Santa Cruz to Cobán.

Rocío's sole job was to comfort Anabella in her delight and terror. Anabella smiled, Rocío noticed, as the moonlight rushed through the holes in the bedroom roof, even as her hands shook so violently that Rocío wondered if her sister weren't having some sort of fit. She gripped her sister's hands tightly under the sheets, pulled them to her breasts, and held them until their trembling subsided. "Tell me," Rocío said.

Anabella said, "Do you wonder what it'll be like? How it will be, when all the guests are gone and I'm in the house with him, just the two of us? What if he doesn't smile?"

Rocío didn't quite follow her, how she had landed at this curiosity, fear perhaps, that Roger Buenafe wouldn't smile. She said nothing but held Anabella's hands close to her until she heard Anabella's whistlelike breathing, signaling sleep. When Rocío closed her eyes, she saw a scene from when she was a little girl and her parents had taken her and Anabella on the only vacation they had ever had, to Livingston, a town on the Caribbean coast, and they had stood on the disappointing shore—disappointing because it was full of broken shells, soda cans, and cigarette butts, not the sweeping sand of her imagination—and had stared across the damp haze to a mountain range far across the water. "That's Belize," her father had said. "It used to be part of our country."

––––––––

The wedding day came, and Rocío helped paint her sister like a billboard advertisement, brushing the deepest black into her eyelashes and rubbing the deepest red on her cheeks and dabbing the whitest white powder on the rest of her face so that from a distance of ten meters Anabella was the most striking creature alive, but from up close she could have walked into a circus without causing a stir among the clowns.

Fully made-up, Anabella looked horrible, which was to say beautiful, and far different from how she had ever looked. She was, at last, not a *gemela* but a bride. From her seat in the second row of the church, Rocío watched her sister walk down the aisle like an angel pulling a cloud.

There was a reception after the wedding on Roger Buenafe's plantation, and the manor house was crowded with everyone from Roger's fellow plantation owners, who came buttoned in blue suits, ties curving out from their chests like the humps on the cattle so many of them owned, to the plantation workers, many of whom, despite their slicked-back hair and clean, white, short-sleeved shirts, smelled as though they had rushed from working in the fields, which many of them had. All the guests shared one thing: sweat. The crush of people and the fact that no one had thought to open a window or two created a high-class desert. Anabella and Roger Buenafe were sitting in a corner of a small, windowless room, and everyone surrounded them, offering congratulations. When Rocío stepped up to kiss her sister, she noticed the makeup running off Anabella like colored raindrops. Her kiss was brief, but long enough to leave the chalky taste of damp powder in her mouth, a taste that remained with her even after she had said good-bye to her sister, both of them too tired and too hot to cry, and had stepped onto one of the buses Roger Buenafe had rented to take everyone back to town. Rocío opened the window and spit, a great glob, into the darkness.

Rocío's bed that night felt like an ocean, and to bear its vast burden, she moved to the edge and slept with one arm dangling off the side.

Opening the bakery the next morning, Rocío didn't notice the sound of the doors but the space inside. The bakery seemed to have grown overnight, and even after serving a dozen customers, Rocío couldn't overcome the feeling that she was alone in a giant cavern. She hadn't imagined her life without Anabella as somber. She had counted on danger, and with it a kind of excitement as she approached undiscovered people and places, but even two weeks later she felt only a dull and disturbing solitude.

Rocío wasn't four days into the school year, which began two weeks after Anabella's wedding, when she got sick. The illness was at first a twinge in her stomach, as if someone inside of it were tickling her. She asked permission of her accounting teacher to leave the room, stepped out of the school and onto the balcony that overlooked the city. Although the pain gripped her like a clawed fist, she couldn't throw up. She tried using the bathroom, one in a row of outhouses fifty meters from the school building that, despite the school's otherwise modern look, remained from years past; nothing happened. She left the outhouse's faintly malodorous but comfortable wood confines convinced that at any moment she would either vomit or soil her pants. She managed, however, to finish the day without incident, although she didn't hear a word any of her teachers spoke. Her mind was fixed on that presence in her stomach, which at times seemed to swell, brushing like broken glass against her insides.

The next day, Rocío remained in bed, although neither her mother nor the nursing student doing her field training in Santa Cruz whom the family knew because of her love of sweet bread— she was always buying dozens of the sugar-topped rolls in the bakery—found a temperature. The nursing student suspected amebas, but after inspecting Rocío's stool that evening, an event that also attracted both her mother and father into the bathroom, she discarded this diagnosis. Amebas made one's stools as "wet as rain in a river," as Rocío's mother said, not like the "concrete blocks" Rocío had produced. Nevertheless, when Rocío's condition persisted the entire week, the nursing student dutifully prescribed ameba medicine, and Rocío took it for the full ten days without the slightest change in her condition.

She was too incapacitated to go to school. She spent four weeks in bed, staring out her window onto the yellow dirt road, watching the wind slap around a rose stem. One morning, she observed from her window a cholera-awareness parade conducted by the junior high, replete with students in skeleton costumes shouting, "*No queremos cólera,*" as if not wanting it would somehow keep it away. By the end of the four weeks, she felt well enough to leave her bed, but she decided she was too far behind in her classes to continue studying, so she volunteered to take both shifts at the bakery until the following school year.

An hour into her first afternoon at the bakery, her mother ran up to her, almost crying, and announced, "Anabella's pregnant!"

The news was not surprising, or shouldn't have been, but it stung Rocío in a thousand places, as if her heart had been overrun by biting ants. Anabella was on the verge of forming her own family, a family distinct from the one she had left. Having failed in her own venture into independence—four days alone at *colegio*—

Rocío was jealous that her sister seemed to be having no trouble at all charging into new territory without her.

Rocío was, however, glad for Anabella, and her happiness was genuine, her smiles real. Having dual feelings about Anabella was not uncommon for Rocío, and within her heart there was no contradiction. Seemingly opposing emotions were like two cars going different directions on the same street. There was a place for both without a collision.

Rocío didn't visit Anabella often. Although there were just a dozen kilometers between their houses, they lived as if on opposite sides of the country. They were reunited for holidays, of course, and on an occasional weekend. And always Rocío was accompanied by her parents, whose deference in Roger Buenafe's presence gave these outings an unpleasantly stiff and formal air.

Roger Buenafe did nothing to help lighten the mood. Everything he did, from overseeing his coffee plantation to sitting down to an afternoon snack of coffee and sweet bread, seemed to require an unbroken seriousness, as if a place in heaven awaited only the austere.

Rocío noticed that Anabella imitated Roger Buenafe's meticulous demeanor; she had given up some of what might be considered her girlish habits, like licking the sugar-coated top off a piece of sweet bread. Now she, like her husband, took dainty bites, delicately trimming the bread, whereas before she had assaulted the crest with her tongue.

There were, however, moments when Anabella left the oppressive dining room — oppressive despite the splendid view of the irrigation ditches cutting wet and crooked through the valley of coffee plants — and Rocío followed her into the kitchen or, as on one occasion, into her bedroom, where the stiffness in her arms and legs seemed to melt, as if she were put together with glue, and her body took on the relaxed pose of a bird falling into a breeze. In the bedroom, Anabella even cracked a hint of a smile, and Rocío felt at home again, like looking into the mirror, and she smiled back. They both laughed at the same time, and Anabella said, "Hello, *gemela*," and Rocío repeated the greeting and they laughed again, hugging each other as if they had been to opposite ends of the world.

Toward the end of her pregnancy, Anabella was confined to bed, where Rocío visited her only once. Roger Buenafe was standing next to the bed like a sentry. Anabella's eyes were open wide, vast like the sky, but like the sky they were far away, and Rocío thought they were this way because Anabella was about to pull another life from them, from that mysterious place, that place beyond the sky where life comes from and disappears.

Their mother stayed on with Anabella, and Rocío returned home to clean and cook for her father. Distraught and dreamy, she burned the tortillas more often than not, and after a week her father, home for lunch, stated as inoffensively as he would critique the weather, "I'm tired of eating ash." Rocío apologized, more profusely than her father seemed to want—he hushed her as if she were, witchlike, reciting an evil incantation—and then she cried, which induced her father into more fervent pleadings of "Quiet, *querida*, quiet." He, too, seemed rattled. Did they know? Rocío wondered later. Did they know, secretly, somehow, what was happening?

Two hours later, Rocío's mother opened the door. Rocío was sitting at the lunch table still, in a sort of paralysis, late for work. Her mother staggered through the door like a drunk, then fell at the foot of the table. Rocío didn't move, stunned, perhaps, by what she somehow knew already. Did she even need her mother's words, wailed from the floor: "Anabella's dead"?

The night after they slid Anabella's coffin into the square slot in the family crypt, sealing it in darkness with concrete dampened further by the rain, Rocío went to bed thinking about the slot next to Anabella's, the six-foot-long cavern that was reserved for the next family member to die. After the mourners left Anabella's crypt, flowers already fading in old tin milk cans beneath it, Rocío had run her hand on the rough concrete walls of the waiting slot, thinking: It's not too cold. In bed, she imagined crawling inside it and having some angel seal her in with the kind of glue that holds clouds together.

When Rocío walked to the bakery, children greeted her with calls of "*gemela*," but if the children were with their parents, their parents shushed them and then addressed Rocío by name. Unsure of their crimes, the children wore dumbfounded looks, and seeing this, Rocío wanted to embrace them and say, "You're right, I *am gemela*; Anabella's here," and then pound her heart.

She tried not to cry—unprovoked tears disturbed people—but she couldn't help herself. The slightest sound, the faintest smell, would set her off. When the *pulman* drove into town or her father carried in a pan of fresh sweet bread, she would burst into tears. She was amazed by her tears, by their prolificacy and power. As she was crying, she often contemplated the abundance and fury of her tears, and she would laugh, and if people were around her, they would gaze at her with concern and ask her if she'd seen a doctor.

Eventually she learned to control her sorrow by thinking of commonplace things—tomatoes and dogs—things everyone saw every day.

Three months after Anabella and her baby died, Roger Buenafe came into the bakery. Rocío had seen him drive by on many occasions. His waxed red Mustang with mud perpetually splattered near the wheels was unmistakable, but his head was always slumped over the steering wheel as if he were sleeping, and he never looked anywhere but straight ahead. Rocío had seen him at the funeral, of course, where, despite his strikingly pale skin, he seemed to blend into the gray drizzle. He would have been invisible except for his dark blue business suit, which made him by far the best-dressed person at the funeral, which most people attended in work clothes, fake designer jeans faded and patched after too much time in the cornfields, or, in the case of the *indígena* women, in white *güipiles* and blue *cortes* that blended into the rainy day without pretense, like a silent prayer in church.

When he stepped into the bakery, Roger Buenafe was in his work clothes, old jeans, boots, and a button-down shirt opened almost to the waist, but despite his casual dress he looked just as stiff and unrelaxed as always. Seeing him, Rocío thought about his reputation as a great basketball player—he sponsored and played for a team in Cobán—yet looking at him, she did not believe it.

How could he protect his dribble while standing as tall and unbending as a tree? There was, however, something dignified in his appearance. His rigidity seemed not just physical but moral. Looking at him made her think of a priest.

They exchanged good afternoons and comments about how long it had been since they'd seen each other. This, however, reminded them of that time, Anabella's funeral, and both fell silent.

"What would you like?" Rocío asked.

"Oh," Roger Buenafe said, as if awaking from a nap, and he asked for twenty sweet rolls.

She put them in a plastic bag and handed it to him.

"You remind me of her," he said.

Rocío frowned, thinking that Roger Buenafe, with all his wealth and education, was no better than her elementary school classmates who, unperceptive or uncaring enough to distinguish her from her sister, called them both *gemela*.

Roger Buenafe seemed to sense her disappointment, and, blushing, stammered, "No, that's not . . ." Then he made an awkward sound, an attempt to laugh that sounded like a puppy's yelp. "That's not what I mean," he said. "I mean, the way you put those rolls in the bag. Well, Anabella used to do it the same way, dropping them in one at a time, like a kid playing with marbles, admiring each one fall."

Rocío blushed, and she couldn't speak. Roger Buenafe was walking out of the bakery before she managed to say something. She called his name, his first name, and this seemed to her a bold and intimate thing, although he was her brother-in-law. He turned, almost spun, like she imagined he would do on a basketball court, a quick move, almost graceful. Flustered, she had nothing more to say, but after a pause he said, "Thank you," and she repeated the words and he left.

They were not *novios*, that was not allowed; they were both officially in mourning, but for the third time that week he came to pick her up at the bakery when she closed it at seven and drove her to Cobán, and they ate dinner at La Posada, the fanciest tourist hotel in town. Again she expressed astonishment at the prices, and Roger Buenafe, looking less burdened than he had the previous two times, said, "This isn't nearly as expensive as restaurants in the capital, that's for sure. I went to lunch once with some friends when I was in my first year in the university and I hadn't been in the capital for more than a week. Well, the bill came and my share was about three times what I had in my pocket, which was about all I had to spend for the rest of the month. Of course I didn't want my friends to think I was a poor boy from the country, which I was, so I went outside and sold my watch to a newspaper vendor. Never ate out in the capital again."

Rocío laughed, really laughed, and Roger did too, but they stopped just as quickly and talked, for the third time in as many dinners, about the night Anabella died.

Rocío had heard the story from her mother, about how, despite the immaculate white room, as sanitary as any hospital room, that Anabella had been staying in on Roger Buenafe's plantation, despite Dr. Alfredo García's around-the-clock attention, despite the rosary, which her mother kept pressing into Anabella's ungrasping hand, Anabella had died, pushing out her dead baby in a river of blood. Anabella continued to bleed after the baby left her, bled so profusely that Rocío's mother wondered if the baby hadn't dragged a machete through Anabella's womb.

Roger, too, mentioned the blood and said that Dr. García, a friend of his from their university days, had overseen hundreds of births but had never seen one quite so horrific and inexplicable as Anabella's. The baby, Dr. García had theorized, might have been positioned incorrectly in the womb.

Despite her outward signs of mourning—the black dress she wore almost every day, clogged with the dust the buses kicked up—despite her real mourning —the pain that seemed to fill her body like liquid and swish around inside her, making her seasick—despite all this, Rocío knew she was falling in love with Roger Buenafe. She suspected, no, knew, that what attracted her to Roger Buenafe were the same things that had attracted Anabella: his hair that he kept long and which, over his left ear, fell in a sweeping curl; his dark eyes buried deep and appearing ferocious until one looked into them, as Rocío had (as Anabella had) and saw that they were not as black as they seemed but were really conglomerations of shades of brown and gray and even, so Rocío decided (so Anabella must have decided), green; and of course, there was Roger Buenafe's height. Roger was about the tallest man in town; he would almost certainly hit his head on the top of the bus if he had to take buses anymore.

There was, too, his wealth, and the glow it threw on her. Being near him was like wearing a crown. Driving in his car—how many times in her life had she been in a car? What was the ratio of times she had been on a bus to times she had been in a car, one thousand to one, perhaps; no, she could not even calculate it, it was like —what did her math teacher lecture about, just before Rocío quit school?—infinity. Driving in his car, she thought, was like flying into infinity.

There were his looks, his wealth. Was that all? Rocío thought. Perhaps that was all; that was a lot, but, no, there was, too, his goodness. She knew he was good because he was so stiff; no evil person carried himself so awkwardly. And she thought about the way he walked as if he had wooden legs—and he played basketball? Not only played but played well, and she wanted to see him play; she wanted, now, to see everything; she wanted, after they were married and the guests had gone, to see if he would smile.

He kissed her, and his kisses were illicit, stolen from Anabella, but not stolen entirely, Rocío thought, like a purse stolen in a crowded market, a stranger robbing another stranger; not stolen entirely, shared almost, but not entirely because Anabella could not bless the arrangement.

Rocío hadn't broken from her sister after all, she realized. She had just come to the path a little later, and she was now walking on it, and the flowers were sweet beside it. But it would end, Rocío knew, in the same darkness that Anabella had found: death, almost certainly death, or if not death then a guilty parting—wasn't she betraying Anabella?—or, perhaps, simple disappointment, Roger Buenafe growing tired of her love. (He had, after all, already traveled this path, and weren't men perpetual wanderers, seeking new paths, despite the flowers?) No, the path led nowhere but to darkness, death, but could she help following it? She couldn't, couldn't turn away from it; it was what she wanted, even the darkness. The slot in the crypt next to Anabella's was rough and cold, but it was hers.

And even as she walked this path, gleefully caressing Anabella's footprints with her own feet, she resented that Anabella had done it all before. Roger Buenafe and Rocío were eating at La Posada for perhaps the twelfth time when Rocío asked, "Did you used to take Anabella here?" She knew the answer of course; Roger Buenafe had probably even told her. But when he said yes, she swept her salad bowl to the floor, and she hardly had time to enjoy its shattering before, crying, she raced out the door and into the drizzle. She didn't get farther than the three steps that led from the hotel to the street before he caught her, turning her around brusquely by the shoulder. "What?" he yelled, as if she had insulted him. "You want something different?"

"Yes," she said. She stared him hard in the eyes, looking to see if, in his chivalry, he would turn nobly away from her rage. He didn't.

He took her hard by the wrist and led her back up the three stairs, through the gaudy reception room with its plush pink chairs and into an open hotel room, just cleaned, a fresh ammonia smell in the air. He closed the door and threw her on the bed. "Now, this is something new," he said, and Rocío began to cry, no longer angry at her sister but missing her, thinking of the bed they had shared and wondering how she could ever have tried to run away from someone she loved, like running away from God.

Roger Buenafe, too, seemed to have changed his mind, and now he was kneeling beside the bed as if in prayer. "I'm sorry," he said, "I don't know what . . . What?" He looked up. "I didn't say anything," she said, sniffling. He took her hand. "I'm sorry," he said.

They held their poses for a long time, long enough for a hotel clerk to come and bang on the door. Roger Buenafe got up to answer, and there was a whispered discussion. When Roger Buenafe returned, he said, "I had to pay for a night. He said we've been in here an hour."

They sat on the bed, kissing. He moved his hand under her shirt, unsnapping, with surprising ease, her bra. "Wait," she thought to say but didn't. She was, again, determined to follow Anabella on this path. Or was it something less than that? Was she simply hungry, not like Anabella or anyone else, or perhaps just like everyone? Hungry, she pulled Roger Buenafe on top of her.

She was not satisfied for long. Roger Buenafe fell asleep beside her, snoring, and she thought about the place Roger Buenafe and Anabella had gone for their honeymoon, Lanquín, where there were caves beside a river where at sundown bats hunted insects and, a few kilometers above the town, a waterfall whose water plunged into a cave and, as far as anybody could tell, went straight to the center of the earth. But Rocío knew that before traveling to Lanquín, Anabella and Roger Buenafe had spent the night in Cobán, undoubtedly in this very hotel, perhaps in this very room. She wanted to be angry, to cry again, but she couldn't, and she let herself see what she was seeing: Anabella, awake on a bed, very much like this bed, as Roger Buenafe was snoring. And she knew what Anabella was thinking, because she thought it too: *His touch is nowhere near as soft as yours.*

Rocío was still supposed to be in mourning, she *was* still in mourning, when her pregnancy began to show. She had felt it first as a dull ache in her gut, like the tickling, nauseating twinge amebas gave her when she had had amebas a few years before. From the beginning, though, she knew what it was, and she threw up in the dead of night, when even her mother was asleep.

She told Roger Buenafe, who offered to marry her immediately, and she was grateful for his offer—it showed his morality (she had been right about that, sort of)—but she declined. She said, "I'm going to die anyway." He ignored her remark, or perhaps he was inspired by it, because he fell to his knees and begged her to marry him. He said that if it weren't for the period of mourning they were both supposed to endure he would have asked her a long time ago. Again, she refused, and she thought to say that if she didn't die, he could marry her. But she didn't say this. She knew she was going to die.

Her parents discovered her pregnancy, or acknowledged it, when her stomach was twice the size of the largest cantaloupe in the market. Both knew who the father was, and the only question

Rocío's father asked was, "Is he going to marry you?" Her parents spent that night beside her bed, trying to convince her to accept Roger Buenafe's proposal. Rocío was, at last, angry. "Didn't you hear me?" she screamed. "I'm going to die!"

Nevertheless, they sent the latest nursing student, an elderly woman named Sylvia, who shared the previous nursing student's taste for sweet bread, to talk with her in the bakery. Sylvia tried, saying, "All little babies need fathers." Sylvia thought it was "ignorant" of Rocío to have a baby without marrying the baby's father who was, after all, willing. Rocío shot back, with as much courtesy as she could manage: "The baby's going to die, understand? And I'm going to die, too."

Roger Buenafe continued to visit her at the bakery. She even let him take her to dinners at La Posada until she started to fall asleep at the table before dessert arrived. Finally, she told him thank you, but she'd rather spend the last days of her life at home.

Her parents and Roger Buenafe were prepared to take Rocío to the hospital at the first sign of trouble, although Rocío said on several occasions, loudly, "I want to die in my own bed."

There was, at last, nothing for any of them to do. Her parents sent her off to work in the bakery every morning, and Roger Buenafe visited her there, his face growing increasingly sadder and more puzzled.

Rocío's water broke well before she was due, at the time of night when even the dogs had gone to sleep, and she didn't even bother to call for help; she decided she could do it, her death, alone. The slot next to Anabella's was rough and cold, but it was hers. Instinct must have made her speak, however, because her mother came into her room. "What did you say?" she asked. "Nothing," Rocío said, but her mother sensed her distress. Before long, her father was in the room, saying, "Felipe"—a neighbor boy—"went on his bike to get Roger. We'll get you to the hospital." "I'm not going," she said, "and it's too late, anyway."

"I'm afraid," she said later, without meaning to; something was pulling her away from the way she wanted to act. "I don't want to die. I love Anabella, but I don't want to die."

"You're not dying," her mother said, smiling a little, "you're having a baby. I did. A lot of people do."

Rocío was angry with this simplistic explanation. Defiant, she yelled, "No, I'm not having . . . I'm dying. I'm dying. There." And she felt a tug at her stomach, like a hand grabbing her insides and clutching. She felt sweat fill her eyes, salty and burning. She closed her eyes. She decided not to open them until she was dead.

She heard a voice, Roger's, she thought: "That blood again." And another, a stranger's voice, a doctor's perhaps, telling her to push, push, push.

It was hard work, she decided, to die. But she really was dying, and she was glad. She'd been right. She felt something move through her like a snake with teeth covering its skin. She heard something cry a long way away. Perhaps, however, it was she who was crying, so she wasn't dead yet. And there was still an immense pain in her, a great something to be rid of before she could die. It was too hard to die. This latest pain was not a snake but a tree, a tree not just in her womb but growing inside her, its hard branches jamming into her heart and hands and touching the back of her throat like a knife. I really am dying, she thought with wonder, and then, delighted, she was dead.

Dead, she heard a pair of voices, crying, and she knew they were hers and Anabella's, voices joyous, high, and unrestrained. She wanted to stop crying, to speak to her sister, but she was too happy to do anything but cry. She felt a soft touch on her left breast and the same on her right—Anabella's hands—and her sister's touch made her stop crying. Rocío reached to take hold of her sister's hands, at last to hold them again, but with each hand she touched something wet, hot, and unfamiliar. "Anabella?" she asked, and opened her eyes.

The Iowa Short Fiction Award and John Simmons Short Fiction Award Winners

1998
The River of Lost Voices,
Mark Brazaitis
Judge: Stuart Dybek

1998
Friendly Fire,
Kathryn Chetkovich
Judge: Stuart Dybek

1997
Thank You for Being Concerned and Sensitive, Jim Henry
Judge: Ann Beattie

1997
Within the Lighted City,
Lisa Lenzo
Judge: Ann Beattie

1996
Hints of His Mortality,
David Borofka
Judge: Oscar Hijuelos

1996
Western Electric, Don Zancanella
Judge: Oscar Hijuelos

1995
Listening to Mozart,
Charles Wyatt
Judge: Ethan Canin

1995
May You Live in Interesting Times, Tereze Glück
Judge: Ethan Canin

1994
The Good Doctor,
Susan Onthank Mates
Judge: Joy Williams

1994
Igloo among Palms,
Rod Val Moore
Judge: Joy Williams

1993
Happiness, Ann Harleman
Judge: Francine Prose

1993
Macauley's Thumb,
Lex Williford
Judge: Francine Prose

1993
Where Love Leaves Us,
Renée Manfredi
Judge: Francine Prose

1992
My Body to You,
Elizabeth Searle
Judge: James Salter

1992
Imaginary Men, Enid Shomer
Judge: James Salter

1991
The Ant Generator,
Elizabeth Harris
Judge: Marilynne Robinson

1991
Traps, Sondra Spatt Olsen
Judge: Marilynne Robinson

1990
A Hole in the Language,
Marly Swick
Judge: Jayne Anne Phillips

1989
Lent: The Slow Fast,
Starkey Flythe, Jr.
Judge: Gail Godwin

1989
Line of Fall, Miles Wilson
Judge: Gail Godwin

1988
The Long White,
Sharon Dilworth
Judge: Robert Stone

1988
The Venus Tree,
Michael Pritchett
Judge: Robert Stone

1987
Fruit of the Month, Abby Frucht
Judge: Alison Lurie

1987
Star Game, Lucia Nevai
Judge: Alison Lurie

1986
Eminent Domain, Dan O'Brien
Judge: Iowa Writers' Workshop

1986
Resurrectionists,
Russell Working
Judge: Tobias Wolff

1985
Dancing in the Movies,
Robert Boswell
Judge: Tim O'Brien

1984
Old Wives' Tales,
Susan M. Dodd
Judge: Frederick Busch

1983
Heart Failure, Ivy Goodman
Judge: Alice Adams

1982
Shiny Objects, Dianne Benedict
Judge: Raymond Carver

1981
The Phototropic Woman,
Annabel Thomas
Judge: Doris Grumbach

1980
Impossible Appetites,
James Fetler
Judge: Francine du Plessix Gray

1979
Fly Away Home, Mary Hedin
Judge: John Gardner

1978
A Nest of Hooks, Lon Otto
Judge: Stanley Elkin

1977
The Women in the Mirror,
Pat Carr
Judge: Leonard Michaels

1976
The Black Velvet Girl,
C. E. Poverman
Judge: Donald Barthelme

1975
*Harry Belten and the
Mendelssohn Violin Concerto,*
Barry Targan
Judge: George P. Garrett

1974
*After the First Death There Is No
Other,* Natalie L. M. Petesch
Judge: William H. Gass

1973
The Itinerary of Beggars,
H. E. Francis
Judge: John Hawkes

1972
The Burning and Other Stories,
Jack Cady
Judge: Joyce Carol Oates

1971
*Old Morals, Small Continents,
Darker Times,*
Philip F. O'Connor
Judge: George P. Elliott

1970
The Beach Umbrella,
Cyrus Colter
Judges: Vance Bourjaily and
Kurt Vonnegut, Jr.

Mark Brazaitis was a Peace Corps volun-
teer and technical trainer in Guatemala
from 1991 to 1993 and 1995 to 1996.
His stories have appeared in the *Sun,
Greensboro Review, Western Humanities
Review, Beloit Fiction Journal,* and other
literary magazines. A native of Wash-
ington, D.C., he teaches English at the
Helene Fuld College of Nursing in
Harlem, New York.